SIMON'S CHRISTMAS MAIL ORDER BRIDE

P. CREEDEN

Sign up for my newsletter to receive information about
new releases, contests and giveaways.
http://subscribepage.com/pcreedenbooks

SIMON'S CHRISTMAS MAIL ORDER BRIDE

This Christmas, love arrives unexpectedly in Douglas County—by stagecoach.

December 1875 – A Christmas dress could bring things together...or tear them apart.

When her world comes apart at the seams, Charlotte Dunn leaves Washington DC behind to become a mail-order bride in Douglas County, Colorado. Sheriff Simon Harris didn't want a wife but can't turn away the stunning dressmaker now that she's here. As a deadly trap closes in around Simon, Charlotte's courage is the only thing that can save her groom and their future. Will her talent with a needle be enough to tailor the perfect Christmas and mend their hearts? Can unexpected Christmas magic spark love's flame between a man with no bride and the woman who has traveled so far to win his wary affection?

This is a clean, wholesome, standalone novella written from a Christian worldview. It has a happily ever after and features down-to-earth characters with real world problems who overcome them by grace and love.

CHAPTER 1

Charlotte Dunn swiped the tears from her face and took a deep breath. She couldn't see through the blur her tears created in order to pin the fabric in a line where she needed to make her stitches. If she continued at this rate, she'd never finish this dress's alterations before the bride came to retrieve it in the morning.

"Charlotte, dear," Mr. Montgomery, her employer, said as he came in and let his hand linger overlong on her shoulder. "It's getting late, and I have an engagement I must attend. Do you think you can close up shop after you're finished with Miss Brown's changes?"

Swallowing the lump that formed in her throat, she nodded. "Yes, sir. I can do that."

"Good." He ran his hand down her arm, caressing it and then giving her a gentle squeeze just above her elbow. Then he leaned in and whispered, causing the hair on the nape of her neck to stand on end, "I'll be off then."

As he turned away, she could control it no longer and shivered. Mr. Montgomery had always skirted the lines between propriety and indecentness. His naturally flirtatious nature made it so that most of his customers felt he was charming and witty, but Charlotte found his behavior quite lecherous, especially since she also knew that he took the money he earned from the beautiful dresses that she made and designed with him and squandered them on inappropriate living and scandalous women.

Concentrating on pushing the pedal of her Singer 12 sewing machine, Charlotte pushed the fabric by the needle. When the model had come out, earlier in the year, she'd been ecstatic that Mr. Montgomery had bought two of the machines hot off the factory floor. With 900 locked stitches per minute, she was able to make alterations and adjustments and sew much faster than the old machine they'd had in the past. But since Charlotte had been working there, Mr. Montgomery's machine hadn't been doing much more than sitting as a trinket collecting dust in the corner, doing no work at all. Instead, her employer spent most of his time attending parties to drum up more customers, wooing the ladies when they came into the dress shop, and taking measurements. Often Charlotte would show Mr. Montgomery her latest designs for wedding dresses and party gowns, and sometimes he would approve and sell them to customers. If she were half as charming as he was, she could open a shop on her own, but as such, she had to make do with what he could do for her. At least he paid her well enough that she could earn enough to support herself and her ailing mother.

Her mother. She let out a deep breath as a pang hit her in the chest. Tears stung the backs of her eyes. Her mother had passed away on Thursday, forcing her to call in sick on Friday so that Charlotte could bury her. It was why she was late on finishing these alterations now. Blinking hard, she allowed the tears to fall for just a moment, and then she swiped them away and got back to work. Work was her life now, and she loved what she did. Right now, she wasn't sure what she was going to do, but she knew that as long as she could sew, she would be just fine.

After finishing up the dress, she put it upon the sewing model where it would be shown to the bride in the morning by Mr. Montgomery. She suppressed a yawn as it came up and she locked the door behind her. The gas lamps overhead had already been lit even though the sun had only begun to set in the mid-October sky. A golden hue surrounded her, making her feel the embrace of the day and giving her the feeling that everything would be all right. The first day back to work since burying her mother had been difficult, but she'd made it through without too much hardship oppressing her. When she reached her home, she ran into Mr. Smith, her elderly downstairs neighbor in the brick brownstone rowhouse where they lived, as he leaned upon his cane. "Hello, Charlotte," the man offered her a gap-toothed grin, but then it settled a bit. "I was sorry to hear about your mother. Are you doing all right? Do you need any help with anything?"

"Thank you for your offer, but I think I'll be just fine. How are you?" She pressed on through the pain that had returned to her with the man's concern and tried to plaster the mask of a smiling young woman to her face. In her heart, she sent up a small prayer asking for help to make it through.

"I'm doing well. But I was wondering if you might do an old man a favor?"

Her eyes widened a bit. "A favor?"

He nodded and stepped inside his doorway, coming back out with a large package, about one square foot in size. "Do you think you might be able to take this to the post office for me? They don't close for another forty minutes."

She blinked at him as she accepted the package that he pushed into her hands. "Now? You want me to take this there now?"

"If you're not too busy," he said and then placed a fifty-cent piece on top of the box. "For the postage."

Her face flushed, but she felt him turn her around and gently guide her back out the door. The breeze had picked up a little outside as she stepped back onto the brick porch of the rowhouse. Then she juggled the box into one hand so that she could take the coin with her other. What was happening right now? Yes. Mr. Smith had a bit of a limp, and it would be difficult for him to deliver the package to the post office himself, especially with so little time before the office closed, but it seemed that he might have done it himself earlier in the day or asked someone else to do it for him.

Regardless, she found herself taking the man's package to the post office, quickly marching through the streets of Georgetown so that she could make it there before it closed. When she arrived, the postman offered her a wide grin. "Miss Dunn, how are you? I was sorry to hear about your mother."

She nodded her thanks and set the package on the counter. Though Washington DC was a great city with a large population, their little neighborhood in Georgetown tended to stay on friendly terms and watched out for each other, especially since there were so many factory and dock workers on their street, and they tended to stick together and support one another well. She set the package on the counter along with the fifty-cent piece. "Mr. Clarke, could you please send this for Mr. Smith? He sent me with the money for postage."

The postman's smile widened. "Of course."

After checking a few things and placing a stamp onto the package and giving Charlotte back the change she'd need to return to Mr. Smith, she began to turn around.

"Hold on, Miss Dunn," the postman called out. "It's been more than a week since you got your mail and you've got a bit of a stack forming."

She blinked. He was right. Because her mother hadn't been doing well and she'd been juggling her work with taking care of Mother, she'd neglected making her way to pick up her mail. But a stack of letters was surprising. The post man offered her six envelopes, which she took with a bit of a confused frown. "Thank you."

He nodded and said, "Welcome. Have a good evening."

After saying her goodbyes, she stepped back outside and started toward home. Out of curiosity, she peered at the letters to see who they were from. Her heart sank as she looked at the return addresses. One was from the funeral home, three were from the hospital and doctors offices, and the other two were just Saturday's weekly and a mailer from Montgomery Ward. Her mother had loved leafing through their catalogues. Frowning, she put them in her leather satchel and continued toward home. Once inside, she stopped at Mr. Smith's door and handed the man his change. When she reached the second floor, the young teenager who lived in the home next door to her stepped into the hallway and looked at Charlotte with sad eyes.

"Miss Dunn," the girl said, her face flushing and her hands wringing. "I was sorry to hear about your mother, and I know that you've been busy with arrangements and work, but did you happen to finish my dress? I'm supposed to wear it to the party tomorrow."

Charlotte's eyes went wide, and she gasped. "Tomorrow is the fifteenth already?"

The girl nodded.

"Oh, Winifred, I'm sorry. I forgot, but come and help me. We'll get it done now," Charlotte said as she quickened her pace and made it to her front door with the girl in tow. She unlocked the door and let herself in, stepping up to the small table beside the door and opened the drawer to get a match. After lighting the kerosene lamp atop the hall table, she ushered Winifred into the room. "Come in. It won't take me long. I'm sorry that I neglected it."

"No, No. I know you've been busy, and it's been such a hard time for you the past few weeks." The girl's sad expression seemed even more drawn in the shadowed light of the lamp.

"Thank you for your consideration, Winifred, but I'm still glad that you reminded me just now." She took the girl's hand and gave it a gentle squeeze. Then she went over to the green sateen dress that was a hand-me-down from her aunt. Charlotte had already put the dress on the girl and pinned it in the right areas in order to make the alterations.

She stepped over to her Singer II, which she'd bought from Mr. Montgomery earlier that year when he'd replaced the ones in the shop, for only forty dollars and had allowed her to make payments. Over five months. She'd only finished paying it off a couple months ago. The machine was slower, noisier, and a bit harder to use than the twelve in the shop, but it was the first sewing machine that was all hers, and for that, it was her pride and joy. After a half hour of work, she was able to send Winifred off with a perfectly fitting sateen dress that she could be proud of when she went to the fall dance she needed to attend. Charlotte was still sad that she couldn't get the work done sooner so that Winifred didn't have to worry about it.

Once the girl left with the dress, Charlotte settled down into a chair at her kitchen table, feeling the sudden solitude she had in the small, one-bedroom apartment she'd shared with her mother. Her stomach growled. Rubbing it, she looked toward her larder and considered what she'd have to make for supper. The motivation to make meals just wasn't there for her anymore. She didn't have her mother to cook for. Right now, her mother would be talking to her or singing hymns between coughing fits. Mother would have scolded her for being so late and for letting everyone ask her for favors and never telling anyone, "No." And her mother would have reminded her that this was why she was always tired.

Letting out a slow breath, a sob wanted to bubble up, but she pushed it back down. She'd done so much crying over the last few days, it was a wonder that she had any tears left. Her eyes fell upon the weekly mailer from last week that she'd left on the table. Inside there was a calling for a mail-order bride agency out west in Denver, Colorado. When things had grown unbelievably bad, there was a part of her that wondered how it might be to escape all of this pain and suffering and loneliness and go west for an adventure. As a teenager, she'd read dime-store novels that told of how the untamed frontier was full of adventure for men, but how would it be for a woman?

She shook her head. Those were foolish thoughts.

Then she remembered the letters that she'd picked up at the post office. They were bills, she knew that she'd racked up some debts in her mother's last days and for the funeral, and that they would come back when due. She also knew that she wouldn't have the money on hand to pay those debts immediately, so she needed to know how much she owed exactly so that she could ask to make arrangements to get them paid.

She pulled her satchel that she'd hung on the

back of the chair around to her and set it upon her lap. After opening it, she peered in and pulled out her stack of mail. Honestly, she didn't want to open the envelopes. She didn't want to eat. She didn't want to get up from her chair and do anything. How was she going to get the strength and motivation to move on from here? She prayed again, hoping that God would help her through these feelings of melancholy. These feelings would have her do nothing but collapse to the floor and cry until morning if she'd allow them to. Either that or just lay there in a numb state until the sunlight came in through the windows. Nighttime was so much harder than during the day. And when she was out and doing things for others, she felt as though she had purpose and could push these feelings aside. But now that she was alone, the melancholy overwhelmed her. How could she be so weak? She should be stronger than this. As a child of God, she knew that her mother was in heaven. She didn't really mourn for her mother's death as much as for her own loss of purpose. Before now, she hadn't realized that she was so selfish. Slowly and with what seemed like more strength than it should have taken she opened up the hospital bills and the bill from the funeral home.

Wincing at each total, she determined to add them all together and figure out how much she'd need to make in order to pay them. Three hundred and thirty-five dollars. That was her total. Her mouth turned dry, and her throat ached. Thirst overcame her, but she didn't have the energy to stand and pour herself some water from the pitcher. How was she going to come up with such a large sum? She had no savings, and she tended to spend every penny of her paycheck on rent and her expenses. Maybe those expenses would be a little smaller now that her mother was gone, but would it really amount to any more than a couple of dollars a week? There was no way that the hospital or funeral home would allow her to make payments so small.

What was she going to do? A sob bubbled up, and for a moment, she went ahead and succumbed to the feeling of melancholy and put her head upon the table and cried. Unsure of how long she'd been crying, she eventually felt dry and empty. And it was then that she finally began to pray.

CHAPTER 2

Sheriff Simon Harris stared at his breakfast, hoping that he wouldn't have to look up again too soon. It was mortifying hearing his sister and his mother talk about him while he sat there trying to eat scrambled eggs that now tasted no better than sawdust.

"I don't understand why he won't just let me send him a bride. Does Simon really plan to spend the rest of his life alone?" Hilary, his sister asked.

His mother chimed in. "I tell him all the time that he needs a wife to help take care of this house. After all, I can't be expected to do it all myself."

"I help too," Simon mumbled around a mouthful of eggs.

They both grew quiet for a long moment, and

Simon imagined that they both had looked at him. But when he didn't look up to meet their glares, they continued their conversation. Simon let out a soft sigh and then downed the remainder of his eggs with a big gulp of his milk. As sheriff of Douglas County, he could stare down rabble-rousers and thieves and troublemakers with the best of them, but when it came to his own mother and older sister— they somehow made him feel like a child again.

"Don't be so stubborn and let your sister send someone to help you," his mother said.

Finally, Simon looked up as he stood. "If you're so bold as to send some unsuspecting lady here to be my bride, Hilary. I will send her packing, even if just to embarrass you."

Hilary's eyes widened. "You wouldn't dare."

"I would." He picked up his plate and mug and took them both to the wash basin. The two women in his life continued to discuss whether or not he would actually do what he said, but Simon had meant every word of it. "I'll be back for supper," he said over his shoulder as he started for the door.

Once outside, he felt as though he could finally get a lungful of air. It was so stuffy and feminine in his house of late. Ever since Hilary had come to Colorado as a mail-order bride, bringing their mother in tow three years ago, his life hadn't been the same. Especially now that they'd both settled in. In order to keep Hilary's new husband happy, Simon had volunteered to take care of their mother, here in Franktown, while Hilary lived with her well-to-do, political husband in Denver. She was only a day's stagecoach ride away, so she came to visit frequently so that their mother could avoid the bumpy ride, herself.

Only thing was that Hilary had become Denver's premiere matchmaker, the owner of a mail-order bride agency that had been serving the city for nearly two years. And that whole time, she'd been trying to get Simon to accept a bride, too. He let out a slow breath as he headed to the stable to saddle up his horse, Nugget. The palomino gelding nickered as soon as he opened the barn door. Simon patted him on the head as he passed to go and get the saddle.

The last thing that Simon wanted was a bride. He'd been in love once. Sarah had been his first and only love. They'd grown up together and went to school together. She was there when his father had passed when he was fifteen. She promised to wait for him, when he'd joined the war between the states on his sixteenth birthday with his best friend, Joe. And then she broke his heart by being married by the time he'd returned at war's end, less than two years later. A man who'd been wounded in the war returned about a month after Simon had left, and apparently, they'd fallen in love while Sarah was helping the doctor care for him in training as a nurse. They were married and she was expecting when Simon had come back.

Distraught and broken-hearted, Simon joined Joe in his pursuit to go west and make a living for himself as a cowboy. They found the Four Mile Ranch in Colorado that would take them on, and Simon had worked there for a little over six months before deciding that it wasn't the life for him, even though Joe thrived in it. Fortunately, Sheriff Grady of the county they lived in was hiring deputies, and Simon went to work for him. Last year, Mr. Grady had retirement forced upon him due to an injury, and appointed Simon as the acting sheriff until the next election, which was coming up on December fifteenth.

He tightened the cinch on the saddle and then slid the bridle over Nugget's head. Once finished, he led the horse outside. Eyeing the house for move-ment, he was half-surprised that his sister didn't come out to bother him again about getting married. He huffed as he mounted and slid into the saddle.

The last thing he wanted to do was end up with his heart broken again. It had taken years for him to stop thinking about Sarah, and now, ten years later, his sister was drudging up all those old memories and the bitterness that clung to them. He reined his horse toward town and trotted away, wanting to open the horse up and gallop away from those horrid thoughts and the sting in his chest that came along, but knowing that Nugget needed to warm up a bit first.

When he made it to town, he stopped in front of the sheriff's office and tied Nugget to the hitching post loosely before stepping inside. He had to blink a bit to get used to the lighting. Before he could even get adjusted entirely, one of his deputies, Marcus, stepped forward. "Sheriff!"

"What is it?" Simon asked.

"Mr. Francis from the Cattleman's Association has asked that you meet him out at the Thompson Ranch. Apparently, there's an incident there."

Simon clucked his tongue, his stomach souring a bit. "Now why did Thompson call Francis out there instead of getting word to me directly?"

Marcus shrugged his shoulders.

Shaking his head, he turned around and headed right back out the door he'd just come in. It had barely shut behind him before he'd yanked it open again. Outside, Nugget nickered at him immediately. His heart softened toward the old gelding. Simon had bought the horse as a barely broke four-year-old back in Baltimore before he and Joe had left to make the ride all the way to Colorado. The gelding had dumped Simon on the ground a few times through that journey, but now they had a bond that couldn't be broken. Simon reached into his pocket and took out a small handful of oats to feed the horse. Then he petted Nugget on the head before untying the reins and mounting in a smooth motion and turning toward the north of town.

It took nearly an hour of good riding before he reached the ranch. He wondered how far behind Mr. Francis he might be when he pulled up at the house and saw the gentleman standing with Thompson on the front porch. He dismounted Nugget quickly and strode over. "Mr. Thompson, good morning. What sort of trouble are y'all having?"

The two men both came down the front porch steps and then gestured toward the barn. "There's something that's been spooking the cattle the last few days and we weren't sure what was going on. We feared a predator was getting too close, but never found any tracks or scat or anything that could let us know for certain. Then late last night, one of the boys caught a trespasser. He claims he's a bounty hunter and wanted to talk to the law. I thought about riding him into town to you, but we only had three of the boys in the bunkhouse last night and the rest are out on the back forty acres working the cattle. I didn't want to risk the man getting away."

Simon lifted a brow toward Mr. Francis. "It doesn't seem like trespassers are the Cattleman's Association's territory."

Mr. Francis smiled wide. "True. True. But, when I ran into Thompson's man this morning before he reached your office, I decided to come and help out an old friend in his time of need. Besides, with Grady gone, some of us don't know if the 'acting' sheriff is reliable just yet."

Tightening his jaw, Simon fought the frown that wanted to surface. Was he really so untrustworthy because he was appointed instead of voted in? He'd only been a deputy in the county for nearly a decade. Instead of voicing his concerns, he nodded. "All right. Show me where you've stashed the trespasser."

Mr. Thompson led Simon and Mr. Francis toward the big barn where they stored injured animals, the cow horses, and they hay that they needed for the winter. The gaps between the boards on the second floor of the building let in enough sunlight that they were able to barely see once inside. A man sat on a milking stool, tied to one of the posts in the middle of the building, with a handkerchief in place as a gag. Simon wondered how long he'd been sitting there like that, considering he'd been caught last night. Stepping forward, he looked into the man's pleading eyes as he pulled down the gag.

The trespasser eyed the star on Simon's chest. "Thank the Lord you've come, sheriff. Is there any way that I could trouble someone for a drink of water? My mouth is terribly dry."

Simon glanced over toward Thompson who nodded to a cowboy nearby. The cowboy returned quickly with a drinking gourd that had come from the nearby well. Instead of untying the trespasser, the cowboy just raised the gourd to the man's lips and offered his drink. After a couple seconds of gulping, the man sighed in relief. Simon finally asked, "What were you doing on the Thompson Ranch, sir?"

The man swallowed again. "The name's Thomas Crowley. I'm a bounty hunter out of Oklahoma Indian Territory."

Mr. Francis and Thompson both made noises of incredulity, and Simon couldn't blame them. "You're a long way from home."

The man nodded. "Yes, sir. I've been following a bandit up this way by the name of Sherman. The clues pointed me the direction of Mr. Thompson's ranch."

"Sherman?" Simon frowned. "What makes you so sure that you'd find him here?"

"Is there any way that you could untie me? My shoulders are sore from having to hold up my arms and I'd like to have a civil conversation if possible."

Simon shook his head. "Just keep talking and we'll think about it. So, what makes you think you'd find this Sherman fella here?"

The man let out a disappointed sigh. "I asked around town in Castle Rock who'd been hiring lately and if any men new to the area had gone calling for a job. Someone at the Cactus Saloon told me about a guy matching Sherman's description here at the Thompson Ranch."

"If that was the case," Mr. Thompson said. "Why didn't you just come to the front door and tell me so? Why trespass?"

At least the man had the decency to look chagrined. "Well, sir, I wanted to make sure that the information I'd gotten at the saloon was correct. I was looking at the cowboys to see if Sherman might be among them first. I didn't want him to get word of my presence and run off."

Frowning, Mr. Thompson shook his head. "Well, the only man I've hired of late is Jack Dillon. And I don't imagine that he's a bandit, as you say."

"I'd like to see for myself, if possible," the supposed bounty hunter said. "Could you ask him to come and meet with me here?"

Thompson nodded toward the cowboy again, and the young man turned on his heel and was out the barn door like a shot. "If you've been looking for him out in the fields the last couple days, you were out of luck. Dillon has been in our bunkhouse resting up. The men spend four days working the cattle and then four day's rest."

"Wise way of working men I suppose," the man said, trying to roll his shoulders while he remained tied.

The young cowboy came running back in, looking pale. "Mr. Thompson! Dillon is gone. It looks like he stole the Appaloosa pony that you had in the west paddock and took off."

Thompson's eyes widened and then he sneered and cursed. "I was supposed to sell that pony to

Brock Ranch as a Christmas gift for Brock's daughter. They paid me a pretty penny for that pony, and I need to deliver it."

Thomas Crowley huffed a laugh. "You see. It was Sherman. Will someone please untie me now so that I can go after him?"

Simon glanced at Thompson who nodded once, the scowl remaining on his face. The young cowboy stepped forward and loosed Crowley's bonds. This time it was Simon's turn to eye the gentleman who looked about ten years his senior. "Do you have your own horse?"

The man nodded. "I do—at my camp about a mile west of here."

"Thompson, could you send a man to go fetch it?"

Thompson nodded again toward the young cowboy.

Then Simon lifted a brow toward the bounty hunter. "I suppose that you can check for tracks and help determine which direction this Sherman might have gone so that we can pursue him?"

Crowley nodded. "Just show me to the Appaloosa's pen."

Simon did the math again. Chances were that this Sherman character had at least two... maybe three hour's head start. He wasn't sure that they'd be able to catch him, especially since he likely went northeast toward Denver. There in the city, the villain could hop on any train heading in any direction. Frowning, Simon didn't care much about that —it was the bounty hunter's problem. What he needed right now was to get back the Appaloosa pony and keep the peace in Douglas County.

CHAPTER 3

Steeling herself, Charlotte stepped toward Mr. Montgomery with her hands fisted at her sides. Even though it was nearly noon, it had been her first opportunity to speak with him since the shop had been busy all morning. "Sir, might I have a word?"

The man looked up from the papers he'd been working on. He'd been working math and numbers in his ledger. "Actually, I have something I need to talk to you about as well," he said, interrupting her train of thoughts immediately. "Starting tomorrow, I've got a new assistant coming in. A second seamstress." He pointed toward the other Singer 12 that had been collecting dust. "It's why I bought two machines a few months back. I've been looking for quite a while and believe I've found the right girl to help. You will give her a hand and take care of her so that she doesn't get lost in the work?"

Charlotte nodded and swallowed down the lump forming in her throat. Part of her had a measure of relief hearing that she'd be getting help, since the shop had gotten much busier than it used to be over the last two years, and she'd been trying to work at a breakneck pace just to keep up with all of the designs and alterations. "I can do that, sir. But I was wondering if I could ask for a favor."

The man's brow furrowed. "What might that be, pet?"

Inside she winced at the term of endearment but tried not to show it outside. She cleared her throat as that lump tried to rise again and close off her ability to speak. The one thing she hated to do was ask for help of any kind. She'd much rather try to get things done on her own than have to ask for assistance. But in this matter, she knew that it would be impossible for her to manage on her own. "Mr. Montgomery, I—"

"Oh please, pet. Call me Claude. Aren't we close enough that you could call me by name and set aside formalities. I may be your employer, but I also consider myself your friend. Of course, whatever it is you need we'll see how we can help in any way possible. But you must call me Claude."

Inwardly wincing again, she said, "Claude, I—"

"You see, that's much better. Now we all feel more comfortable."

No. She didn't feel more comfortable at all, and if he kept interrupting her, she'd never be able to get out what she needed to say. Somehow it seemed that he never let her get a word in edgewise, so she rarely even attempted to speak with him. But now she needed to. And her frustration at trying so far was making her angry. That wasn't what she needed right now. If she got angry, she'd start to cry and she didn't want to show her employer that kind of emotion while she asked, "Sir, I need a loan if I might ask for one."

His brow lifted higher, and the slightest sneer lifted one of his lips. "A loan? This is about money?"

"I'm sorry, sir. It's just that I have hospital expenses and the funeral home needs—"

"Funeral home! My goodness, poppet. Why would you be talking to a funeral home? Who has died?"

Charlotte was unused to sharing about her personal life with Mr. Montgomery as he was difficult to talk to. Her voice cracked, and she looked down at her feet as she answered, "My mother."

His lips thinned, and he rested a hand on her shoulder. "Oh, I'm so sorry to hear about that, pet."

Then he ran his hand up and down her arm gently, making her feel uncomfortable. She swallowed the bile that was rising in her throat and stepped to the side a bit. "The hospital and the funeral home are asking to be paid, but I don't earn enough to do so at once. Is it possible for me to get a loan? I could pay it back over time."

Mr. Montgomery frowned and looked disapprovingly at Charlotte for a nearly a minute. And as she waited, her heart began to sink as she became certain he wasn't going to approve. Then his eyes flashed as though he'd had an idea. "How much money do you owe, poppet?"

Hope sparked in her heart. "Three hundred and thirty-five dollars."

A small bit of surprise and anger seemed to flash across his face, but he kept his expression, stepping toward her and putting his hand back on her shoulder. "I can pay that then, poppet. Let me take care of those bills for you today. But, you know that you'll have to do me a favor soon. All right?"

"What kind of—"

"Nothing to worry your pretty little head about right now," he said as he touched her on the nose. He was too close and seemed to be getting closer. "Just point me in the direction of your debt and I'll take care of it all today."

Something deep inside Charlotte told her not to do it. That she shouldn't expect this to come at a low price. Somehow, Mr. Montgomery was going to ask her for something of value in addition to expecting her to pay the debt over time. But she let out a slow breath and succumbed anyway, giving the man the envelopes that contained the bills, her shoulders dropping as she did so.

"Not to worry, poppet," he said as he took them and tapped them against the top of the counter and then started for the door. "I'll be back after paying these. You take care of the shop in my absence. Understood?"

"Of course," she called out. The bell over the doorway rang as the door tapped against it. And then he was gone. She had hoped to feel some measure of relief when she'd talked to Mr. Montgomery about the money, but instead, she continued to feel unsettled. His promise of a favor made her as uncomfortable as the man's lecherous touch. What could he possibly ask of her though that wouldn't be worth getting rid of her debt? Part of her was afraid to ask that question, because she knew it might be more than she was willing to give. Still. What choice did she have?

AT THE LIVERY CLOSEST TO THE TRAIN STATION IN Denver, Simon found the Appaloosa that he was looking for. He ended up having to pay the livery owner for the fee for keeping the pony for the past couple of hours, and then he checked in with Crowley, who had found that his man had taken the first train out, which happened to dead end in Boulder and wouldn't be leaving again until morning, so, if he continued to ride hard for a few hours, he might be able to catch him there. So, the bounty hunter said his goodbyes and Simon started the ride home, ponying the Appaloosa.

After dropping it off at the Thompson Ranch, and getting reimbursed for the livery fees, he continued on into town as the sun began to set. His stomach grumbled at him. It had been a long day, and the exhaustion was just hitting him at the same time he'd realized he hadn't eaten a thing since the scrambled eggs that morning. Frowning, he concluded he was going to be a bit late for dinner as well. He hated making his mother wait for him. Because he was a lawman, she often worried about him being harmed in the line of duty.

"Sheriff!" A gruff but shrill voice called out to him.

He turned around in his saddle and found Mrs. Francis waving her fan his direction. Heaving a bit of a sigh, he reined his horse up and then quickly dismounted so that he could greet her. "Evening, ma'am. What can I do for you?"

A wide smile spread across her face. "I'm just heading home after a meeting with my bridge club, and we were discussing how the election is coming up."

He nodded, knowing that the ladies in the bridge club were all somewhere between Mrs. Francis' age and his mother's, and made up a lot of influence among the voters in Douglas County. "That's nice. How was the game?"

"It went well," she said, preening like a schoolgirl. "I won. Well, anyway, we were discussing how there is a rumor going about that Mr. Jeb Holt of Castle Rock might also be running for the seat of Sheriff of Douglas County."

His heart sunk a little, but he kept his face impassive. "Is that so?"

She nodded. "As a family man, he may have a better chance of garnering the vote. His family has been around since the Gold Rush of 1860, and they've got deeper roots in the community."

And that made his heart sink a little more. "But I've been working in the sheriff's office myself since '65."

She nodded. "That might be so, but you're still very young and don't have family roots to keep you here. The ladies and I all agreed that it would be better if you were married."

And now there felt as though a dagger were sticking out of his heart. "Married?"

"I know it's hard to find a good Christian woman of marrying age around these parts. Even Denver has a bit of a shortage. But I hear-tell that your sister runs a matchmaking agency. Perhaps you should consider..."

He nodded as that dagger twisted a bit, but he straightened and stiffened his spine. "I understand. Thank you and the ladies for your lovely advice. I'll have a word with my sister."

"All right," she said with a smile. "I'm glad we could be of help. Have a lovely evening."

"You, too," he said as she waved and started away. It took a long moment for him to catch his breath. He rubbed the center of his chest where his heart hurt. He'd not thought of how it would be if he didn't win the election and remain sheriff in Douglas County. Since he'd already been acting sheriff, if a new sheriff came in, they'd likely clean house, and get rid of all the current deputies, replacing them with men of their own in order to be sure of getting loyalty. He felt a little sick as he thought about Marcus and the other deputies not having work or places to go either. They were good men... good lawmen and they didn't deserve to be cast to the wayside just because a new sheriff had taken over. And who exactly was this Jeb Holt? Simon hadn't heard of him, but he'd not been called out to Castle Rock much either.

Frowning, he shoved a foot into his stirrup and mounted Nugget. A marriage would appease the bridge club ladies, but would it truly appease anyone else? He supposed that it might do him more good than harm, as far as the election was concerned. Turning toward home, he had a hard time not feeling sick. Was he really considering marriage to appease his constituents? What would he do, himself, if he no longer had work as the sheriff or as a deputy in Douglas County? He didn't want to lose the home and the life he'd built here. Sure, he wasn't very old yet, but he'd spent more than a third of his life in the county and loved it here. He had no intention of leaving. But without family roots, how could he prove it to the voters?

It was so frustrating. He didn't want to get married. He didn't want to set himself up again for heartbreak. But he also didn't want to figure out what to do again with his life if he lost the ability to be a lawman. And he didn't want for his deputies to be ousted either. Turning toward home, he knew his mother was going to be upset with him for coming so late, but he now had news that would cheer her quickly. He didn't have to take a bride in every sense. Perhaps he and his bride could just make some sort of arrangement. They could be married and live in the same house without actually having to be in love or having affection for each other, right? Perhaps they could make it work. Nodding, he pushed Nugget forward into a lope. The sooner he got this all over with, the better. He could only imagine his sister's smug face when he told her to go ahead and send him a mail-order bride.

CHAPTER 4

"There, poppet. It's all done," Mr. Montgomery said as he swept back into the shop three hours later and set the papers on the table in front of her.

Blinking, Charlotte picked up the bills and found them all stamped with the word "paid" on them in red. She felt a sob bubble up as relief hit her hard. Looking up from the papers, she found Mr. Montgomery beaming at her. Swallowing back the sob and voice cracking, she said, "Thank you so much, sir."

"Oh hush, pet," he said as he came over and pulled her into his side. He smelled strongly of Bay Rum, and the spicy-citrus scent tickled her nose. "You must remember to call me Claude. No more sir or Mr. Montgomery. And tonight, we will be attending a gala. I need you to wear that violet purple dress with the lace."

Her eyes widened as she attempted to pull away a bit and look up at him, but he held her tight. The dress he'd referred to was one she'd designed and made of satin and had a bustle and a bit of a train. She'd never even thought to have worn such a fancy thing. And a gala? Why would he be taking her to such a place? She was just a plain seamstress without any family or breeding or training in how to behave at events. How was she going to manage? But somehow, she couldn't voice any of her concerns. Mr. Montgomery had already squeezed her hard and released her and then started going on and on about who they were going to see and how the hotel would be decorated and how people were going to respond to that purple dress that he'd designed—for he always took credit for her designs as if he'd come up with them himself.

She let out a slow breath and thought to herself that she needed to just do as he asked and get it over with. With every intention of paying the man back for taking care of her bills, she knew that she just needed to appease him for allowing her to pay over time instead of all up front like the hospital and funeral home needed her to do. Maybe all Mr. Montgomery needed was a guest that would make him not look alone. Most of the trollops that he spent time with wouldn't be the kind that you would take to a grand party like this one. And once this gala was over with, she hoped that would be the only favor that he would ask of her and she'd be able to continue on paying him back and living her normal life.

But, she couldn't have been more wrong.

That evening, the first time Mr. Montgomery introduced her as his beloved fiancé, she was struck with wordless shock. But it wasn't to be the only time. Over and over again, he introduced her as such, and it came to the point where she'd feared she would embarrass him if she corrected him. So, she went through the evening allowing the lie to continue and perpetuate. And by the end of the evening, she was exhausted. When they were finally alone again on the walk back toward her home, which he insisted upon escorting her, she took a moment to correct him. "We shouldn't really lie in such a manner. It's unbecoming."

He lifted a brow, continuing to walk forward under the gas lamps as the October breeze blew around them. "Whatever do you mean, poppet?"

Frustration within her grew as she pulled her shawl tighter around her. "Why did you tell everyone that I was your fiancé?"

That made him stop dead in his tracks, but they were in shadow, so she couldn't read his facial expression as he turned toward her and said, "Because you are, my darling."

Her heart sunk in her chest. She wanted to deny him, but confusion still clouded her mind and made her slow to think.

"Did you think that I would just pay someone's— anyone's debts? I told you that you would owe me a great deal when I took care of those for you. So, you will pay it back with the remainder of your life—as my wife and my seamstress. I'll be able to reach higher echelons of society as a married man than I ever could as a bachelor. Even today I garnered an invitation to the mayor's house for a dinner party. And what greater way do I have to ensure that you will remain with me and not join another dress-maker than to seal our bond with marriage vows, my pet?"

How could he have made himself clearer? She took a step back. "But I intend to pay you back every penny that you spent on my debts."

Stepping forward, and closing the space between

them, he took hold of her arm firmly but not forcefully and then he stroked her cheek with his other hand. "Oh, my pet. No need to worry yourself over trivial little matters. I had a plan for you from the beginning. You will have no worries about money or debts, for you and I will climb the ladder of Washington society together and make dresses at twice the price we do now. It will be perfect."

"Perfect?"

For a moment, she froze because she saw the gleam in his eyes as he stepped out of the shadows and into the light of the gas lamp nearby. His eyes were like those of a predator, and she was the prey. Fear overcame her for half a second before it was replaced by something else. Anger. How could this man just make the assumption that she would do as he asked? He'd never even given her the option to marry him but had bought her instead as soon as the opportunity arose. She was not some harlot that he could purchase to do what he wanted with. And a vision flickered through her mind of what life would be like with this lecherous man as her husband and her spending the rest of her life silent as he walked all over her. She refused to sit quietly by and let that future become a reality.

"No," she said firmly as she yanked her arm away

and stepped away from his hand upon her face. "I refuse to marry you."

Anger flashed through his eyes and his nostrils flared. "You what?"

"I will not marry you."

This time he stepped forward and grabbed her arm hard enough that each of his fingers dug into her skin and she feared that her bone might crack. A cry of pain escaped her and tears stung the backs of her eyes, but through it all she saw the malice and evil intent shining in his eyes. For the first time, she worried for her own life.

"Hey!" A voice called from not too far away. "Now see here! Unhand the lady at once."

Even while he still grasped her arm, they both turned toward the sound. Mr. Smith was walking with his police officer son, along with Winifred and both of her parents. Relief overcame her at the sight of her neighbors.

The younger Mr. Smith stepped forward as an officer of the law. "What do you think you are doing," he commanded. "Release the lady, now."

Blinking, Mr. Montgomery released her arm and backed away a step. "Forgive me, officer, it was just a minor misunderstanding between myself and my beloved fiancé. Nothing untoward happening here."

"Fiancé?" The elder Mr. Smith asked, his brow furrowed.

Finally, Charlotte found her voice. "Absolutely not. I am not his fiancé, nor do I want to be. He became violent when I refused his offer of marriage."

Hissing, Mr. Montgomery glared at her. "Poppet, this is not the time or place to air out our grievances. Can we not discuss this later, when we are in private?"

"I will not be anywhere in private with you ever again," Charlotte said, rubbing her arm where the man's fingers had been. She knew that if she'd ever allow him to be alone with her again, that malice and evil import would come out again and she'd indeed fear for her life once more. "Please take this as my notice of intent to end my employ with you."

His brow lifted and he huffed a mirthless laugh. "Really? You think that you'll be able to work in this town again? When word gets out how you robbed me of my money and left me in a lurch like this that anyone will hire you? Think again!"

She shook her head. "You paid those debts of your own free will and even took care of them in person, so those people will know that I did no such thing. And besides, I've told you over and over that I would repay you."

"Lies!" A look of pity filled his eyes. "Poor little poppet. You'll be living in nothing but poverty and I've already told you that I found your replacement. Who do you think they'll believe? You or me?"

Swallowing hard, she wasn't sure what to say. The bluster and strength she had a moment before had suddenly left her and she felt a bit deflated.

"I believe her," Little Winifred said, coming and looping her arm with Charlotte's.

"I believe her, too," Mrs. Shoe, Winifred's mother, said as she looped into her other arm.

"As do I," Officer Smith said as he stepped between her and Mr. Montgomery, glaring in the man's direction.

"Bah!" Mr. Montgomery said, waving his had dismissively and turning away. He didn't turn back but stomped away in his anger.

Relief flooded Charlotte as she blinked and allowed the tears to fall down her face. "Thank you so much," she said, feeling their love and support. "I don't know what would have happened if you all hadn't stepped in."

"Think nothing of it," elder Mr. Smith said as he came up and rested a hand on her shoulder. "You are a part of our neighborhood, and we wouldn't let someone abuse you in such a way. The nerve of that man."

"You'll be fine," Mrs. Shoe said. "Trust the Lord. God has a plan for everything, so that when one door shuts, another opens—you'll see."

Winifred squeezed her arm. "Just have faith. We believe in you."

The overwhelming love she felt from her neighbors helped carry her home without feeling much worry. But once she arrived at her apartment in the rowhouse, alone, the weight of everything that had happened fell upon her shoulders. What was she going to do now? How was she going to live and pay rent without a job to support herself? She collapsed in a chair at her kitchen table and looked down again at this week's mailer. The mail-order bride advertisement flitted across her mind. Maybe she'd answer it. Maybe someone out there would want a shunned seamstress, like her. Denver and that world were a thousand miles away from Mr. Montgomery and his influence.

A fresh start.

A place where memories of her mother didn't haunt her in an empty home. Where people didn't know who she was or what her reputation might become. That sinking feeling was coming over her again. If she succumbed to it, she'd collapse on the floor in this beautiful violet satin dress and cry. Taking a deep breath, she closed her eyes and prayed—thanking God for the escape that he'd provided and that things didn't end up worse than they did. She thanked God for helping her out of Mr. Montgomery's workshop, because the reality was that it wasn't the best place for her to work anyway. She thanked the Lord that He had helped her formulate a possible means to a fresh start too. And when she felt better, she put pen to paper and began writing a letter to answer the mail-order advertisement.

IT WAS A WEEK LATER WHEN SIMON SENT HIS SISTER back to Denver in a stagecoach, grinning like a cat who'd gotten into the cream. "I'll be sending back a bride very soon."

His stomach soured at the thought. "Don't be in too much of a hurry, and don't just send any girl. You better vet her like you do for all your clients. This is for your business, so a successful match would behoove you, would it not?"

Waving her hand dismissively, she shook her head. "Of course, dear brother. Rest assured that I will not be sending you just anyone. The girl you receive will be special. I'll send word when you should expect her."

"No rush," he said through gritted teeth. She and his mother were enjoying this situation far too much. What they didn't know was that he had absolutely no intention of having a real marriage with the woman. He just needed to put on a good show for the voters.

His mother and sister embraced each other and then Hilary mounted the carriage. She waved from the window as the stagecoach pulled away. It had been a long visit, and in some ways he was happy to have some semblance of normalcy back in his life, but he was sad to see his sister go. Of course, a two-week visit had only been possible since her husband was away on a trip to Washington DC for a meeting on making Colorado into a state rather than a territory. They hoped to make that happen before the end of the year. He was due to arrive home in a day or two, and Hilary wanted to be back there in order to prepare and greet her husband properly.

As the carriage pulled around the bend and out of sight, a horse and rider was approaching through the dust. Simon frowned. He couldn't recognize the horse or rider as someone from town, and it was odd as he noticed that the rider had another person laying behind his saddle. While the rider continued to approach, Simon ushered his mother into the nearest shop which happened to be the millinery. "You were needing a new hat for Christmas, weren't you, Mother? Go ahead and have a look."

"Oh, really. It won't take up too much time?"

"It's no problem. Take your time and pick out the right one. I need to take care of something and then I'll return to fetch you."

"All right then," she said as she stepped into the hat shop.

Simon stepped back outside just as he was able to finally recognize the horse and rider. It was the bounty hunter, Tom Crowley again. The rider approached, and Simon eyed the person over the back of the horse. "Looks like you got your man. Hopefully the bounty was dead or alive."

Pulling up his horse, Mr. Crowley doffed his hat and wiped his brow before replacing it. "Believe it or not, I found him that way. I had nothing to do with his demise."

Simon lifted a brow, finding that hard to believe.

"It seems that the man who hired him for a job caught up with him and now this is what's left."

"What sort of job might that be? Was it local? Something I need to concern myself about?" Simon asked, feeling a bit of unease at the thought.

"Mr. Sherman here was a bank and stagecoach robber. When he got to Boulder, he attempted to bully himself onto a stage. That went south, and he ended up getting arrested. Someone shot him through the bars to the prison from the window outside." Then Tom lifted a brow, himself. "I was with the sheriff at the time, seeing if he'd let me take custody and deliver him to a marshal. We both heard the gunshot. You see; I have an alibi."

Frowning, Simon said, "Banks and stagecoaches. I think both of them have been fine here in Franktown. Hadn't heard much about that at all here in the county. Are you done here, then? Moving on back toward Indian Territory?"

The man shook his head. "I'm delivering this one to the marshal, who happens to be over in Castle Rock conducting business. I didn't feel like waiting around for him in Denver."

"You didn't have to come back through here to get to Castle Rock," Simon said with a frown.

"I know," Crowley said. "It's just that I wanted to

give you a warning. There's been a rash of robberies in the counties surrounding Denver of late mostly north and west so far, and this Sherman was just the tip of the iceberg apparently. He was telling the Boulder sheriff all about how there were other men involved and how the leader of the ring he joined up with was a local man, but liked to hire out-of-towners like Sherman. The criminal was trying to make some kind of deal with the sheriff and the prosecutor to get a reduced sentence if he sang like a bird and gave them all the names and plans that he knew about. That's when he was shot before he could sing."

Worry knotted in Simon's stomach. This was not the kind of news he needed to hear. Slowly, he nodded. "Is there anything that I can do for you Crowley?"

The man shook his head and turned his horse down the east facing street. "That's it for me. After I drop this one off I'm hoping to head home. If I hear anything else significant that might affect you, I'll send you a telegram."

"I appreciate it."

The man nodded and then trotted off, the body of Sherman bouncing on the back of the sorrel gelding, and it was a wonder that the horse didn't have a bucking fit for the discomfort of carrying the extra weight.

Just then, the bell on the door behind him rang as it was opened. He turned about to find his mother stepping out of the shop wearing a new red hat with a sprig of holly on it. She gestured toward it in a flourish. "Very festive, is it not? I put it on your tab."

A small smile tugged at his lip. "Very festive, and perfect for you mother. It's beautiful and I don't mind paying to enhance your beauty."

"Oh hush," she said, waving at him to quiet down but smiling wider.

"Will you wear that lovely hat home?"

She shook her head and held up a box. "Hold this for me?"

He held the round box for her as she pulled off the lid. There inside was the bonnet she'd been wearing earlier. She pulled out the bonnet and set it in her elbow while she unpinned the holiday hat she'd been wearing and placed it in the box. Simon put the lid back on the box while she tied her bonnet under her chin. Then he offered her an arm. "May I escort you home now, Mother?"

"Directly," she said with a smile as she took his elbow.

His mind whirled while he walked his mother to

the livery to fetch their wagon. Bank robberies and stagecoach hold ups and all in and around Denver. The boss of the operation was a local man hiring out-of-towners and was brazen enough to shoot a witness all the way in Boulder. This wasn't good, and he couldn't help but wonder why he'd not heard much about this situation before. And what made Douglas County different that it hadn't yet been affected by the robberies. As they passed the bank, he eyed it. Perhaps they were just next on the list. That thought sobered him and he couldn't help but mull on it as he drove his mother home.

CHAPTER 5

I t was barely a week later that Hilary sent word that Simon would be expecting the arrival of his bride the very next day. Frowning at the telegram again, he sat at the breakfast table with his mother across from him, preening and smiling wider than he'd seen her do in years. He pointed his fork at her. "You're enjoying this a bit too much, you know that?"

She danced a little in her chair. "I don't know," she said. "I believe that I am enjoying this just the right amount. And it's rude to point."

He let out a little sigh and put his fork back down on his plate. Maybe he'd gotten too used to dealing with only men, and many of them criminals. He'd lost some of his social graces over the years, he supposed, and now that he had a wife due to arrive shortly, he'd need to gain some back again. "You're right. I'm sorry."

Waving a hand in front of her face, she huffed a laugh, her smile unfaltering. "I twisted my ankle a bit coming up the back porch steps getting eggs this morning. Could you meet the new lady on your own today?"

"Are you sure you don't want to come? I could carry you to the cart."

"Hogwash!" She said with her brow furrowing for the first time. "I will stand on my own two feet when I meet my new daughter-in-law, and I want to rest my ankle until she comes here. That will help it."

Somehow he doubted that there was anything actually wrong with his mother's ankle. But he wasn't sure what the reason was exactly that she wanted him to go and meet her alone. Then he realized with a slow nod. His mother wanted for them to meet alone and spend the first few moments of getting to know each other while unchaperoned. Of course she did. He pulled out his pocket watch and downed his milk before standing. "I guess I'm off then, the coach is due to arrive in about an hour. I'll be back in two hours or so."

"Take your time," she said, standing and taking up both plates before turning to the wash basin. "I'll be cleaning and straightening up a bit before she arrives. Don't want anything to look in disarray, especially since your sister and I spent all that time while she was here making sure this place was spotless. I can't remember a time..."

At some point in conversations, Simon just couldn't pay much attention anymore. There were times when he could barely get his mother to speak, and other times when she wouldn't stop talking enough for Simon to tell her that he needed to go. This was one of those times. While she was yet speaking, he shoved his hat on his head and started out the back door. "I'll see you in a bit, mother."

"Of course, dear!" She called out, and he was half-surprised that she'd even heard him over her own rambling.

After he got Nugget harnessed and attached to his cart, he drove to town with the November breeze swirling around him. Maybe it was good that his sister had sent him a bride so swiftly, with the election coming up in a little over a month. At least his new bride would have time to settle in and meet some of his constituents so that they could see that he'd started to get roots in. Most of the trees along the lane had lost more than half their leaves, but the ones that still clung to spindly branches were red, yellow, and orange in color. The leaves strewn across the path almost made it seem that it had been cobblestoned with multi-colored rocks. Scents of the dirt and wetness filled his nostrils as his horse helped the process of decay by crushing the leaves under hoof.

November should have had the opposite saying as the one for March he'd heard growing up. "In like a lamb and out like a lion," was much truer for November there in Colorado than it had ever been for back home in Maryland. Winters here in the west were harder, but the summers were much more pleasant. He supposed that's the way life always needed to be, since God gave rain to both the godly and the ungodly the same. People were always going to have to choose to give up one good thing to gain another.

But how was this true besides when a man was dealing with the weather or what state to live in. What good thing was Simon going to have to give up in order to gain this partnership he was heading into? Well, he knew he'd have to give up being a bachelor, but that wasn't really something he worried about much. And having a new woman in his life to support and nag at him—he already took care of his mother, so he could handle that as well. What other things would he have to deal with, he wondered as he pulled his horse to a stop at the hitching post near the stagecoach office. He checked his pocket watch before dismounted the carriage. The coach was due to arrive at eight a.m., and his watch declared he still had four minutes. Looking down the lane, he couldn't yet see any sign of its coming.

"Sheriff!" Mrs. Francis called and waved her handkerchief at him.

He quickly hitched Nugget to the post before striding over to her. "Good morning, ma'am. What can I do for you today?"

She lifted a brow at his cart. "There's a rumor going around that you're expecting a bride to arrive on the coach this morning."

Frowning, he nodded slowly. How had Mrs. Francis heard about it? His jaw tightened. Had it been his mother? But she'd been home all day since they got the telegram, cleaning and getting things ready. Or maybe Mr. Carpenter, the telegraph operator. Much more likely. As far as he knew, those were the only two who even knew about her arrival. He let out a resigned sigh. "Yes, ma'am."

She stepped closer as though trying to bring him into her confidence. Looking around, she said quietly, "I know that the Bridge Club and Temperance League both wanted you to be married before the election, but perhaps bringing in a mail-order bride wasn't the best of ideas after all."

Blinking at her, he frowned. Wasn't he doing the very thing that she'd suggested? "Why do you say that?"

Her own frown tugged at her lip. "Not that we ladies have any problem with it, but the word around the barbershop is that you're getting a mail-order bride because no one in town or nearby would do because you're too sour to find a woman to want you. That you're bringing in a stranger because no one who knows you for long would want to be married to you. They're joking that you're going to rush your bride straight to the altar before she has the time to find out."

His heart sank toward his stomach. Nothing that he could do would make things right for these people. No matter how many hoops he jumped through, he wasn't going to jump through enough for anyone. Letting out a measured breath, he looked up toward heaven. He shouldn't have been trying so hard to please people. Instead, he should have just relied upon God and worked only on pleasing Him. If he lost the job as sheriff, then fine. God would provide something better. He knew that and believed it to be true, and yet he'd allowed the fear of the future to make him jump into doing something that he didn't want to do. Now what would he do about it? "Is that right?"

"I don't think it's right, but that's the word as I heard it from Mr. Francis, and the word has made it around the Cattleman's Association as well."

"What do you suggest I do about it? Would it please everyone if I just went ahead and sent her on back to Denver?"

Her eyes widened as she shook her head. "No, sir! Quite the contrary. I'm certain the rumor would then become that she took one look at your surly frown and decided to rush back home of her own accord." Her hands went to her hips. "I'm not sure what should be done, maybe nothing. But I wanted to let you know what was going on so you were not caught unawares."

"Thank you, then," he said as dust was kicked up down the street and he knew the stagecoach was on its way before he could even see the horses.

"Whatever you decide to do will be fine," Mrs.

Francis said, taking hold of and squeezing his elbow as she started past. "I'll pray for you."

"Thank you," he said again as she walked away, and the stagecoach pulled around the bend and came into view. His frown deepened.

This was all a mistake.

Not only was it wrong for him to try to appease his constituents, but it was wrong for him to have dragged this poor, unsuspecting young lady into the middle of this mess. Now she was going to have to deal with rumors and judgement before she'd even dismounted the carriage. He shoved his hands into the pockets of his dungarees. How was he going to fix this situation?

The six dark horses pulled up beside him, so close that the first one could reach out his nose and nearly touch Simon on the shoulder. He came around the side to await the young woman his sister had sent. Butterflies formed in his stomach. He hoped she'd be plain—or rather, just pretty enough that people would think—What was he doing? There he was, caring again about what other people thought. It didn't matter what she looked like any more than it mattered what people thought. He needed to focus on pleasing God and being himself. He needed to trust that God had a plan for his life.

His heart was much too wishy-washy and he hated that about himself.

Lord, please help me, was all that he could manage to think before the coachman hopped down and put a step stool out for the people disembarking from the carriage.

The coachman opened the door and held out a hand to help a young lady down who was wearing a purple traveling dress with a tan cloak. She stepped down from the carriage, and Simon's heart skipped a beat in his chest. Was this the lady his sister had sent? She peered around her, but hadn't yet looked Simon's direction, and a smile played upon her lips that lit her face. And Simon feared he might melt, right there upon the spot. She was the most beautiful creature he'd ever laid eyes upon, and then her gray-eyed gaze fixed on his. That smile she'd had a moment before was soft and relaxed, but she smiled wider in greeting as she stepped forward and offered a gloved hand. "Sheriff?"

Simon nodded, feeling a bit dumb. He cleared his throat in hopes that it would loosen his tongue as he took her hand. "I'm Sheriff Simon Harris. It's a pleasure to meet you Miss..."

"Charlotte Dunn," she said as she squeezed his

fingers cordially. "Mrs. Eaton from the agency sent me."

It still was strange for Simon to hear of Hilary referred to by her married name. "Right. She sent me a telegram."

She nodded as he released her hand.

Heat rose up his neck. Why was it so embarrassing to talk to her? She was just like any other lady who'd come to town that he was sent to greet. Only this time, she was here to visit him—visit? She was here to marry him. He let out a slow breath. But did he even want to get married? "I have a cart this way," he said as he took her carpet bag. "Do you have a steamer trunk?"

She nodded. "I actually have two."

His eyebrows went up a bit. She'd have had to pay extra for the second trunk both for the train and for the stagecoach. What could be so valuable that she'd need a second trunk? "Two?"

Her brow creased with worry as she nodded. "I'm a seamstress and a dressmaker. My neighbors and friends helped me pay for the second trunk to hold my sewing machine."

"Oh," he said in surprise as he nodded. "That is completely understandable then. My mother also used to work as a seamstress while I was growing up."

It was good to know that his new bride-to-be wasn't just a vain woman with tons of clothing and trinkets, but a working woman who had friends and neighbors who cared for her in the past. Perhaps her neighbors here in Douglas County would feel the same? He could only hope.

"Sheriff," Mr. Carpenter and his wife greeted them with a nod as they walked by, the gentleman eyeing Miss Dunn and lifting his brow in a knowing way.

Another sigh escaped Simon. How was he going to make something out of this mess? He set the carpet bag in the back of the wagon and then returned to get the two trunks.

IT HAD SURPRISED CHARLOTTE HOW HANDSOME THE sheriff was. She was expecting a rugged man, and though the sheriff was, he also had a soft kindness about him. Relief had flooded her the moment she saw him, and she couldn't help but be happy for it. Mrs. Eaton had told Charlotte that she was being sent to her own brother, the sheriff of Douglas

County. Assured by Mrs. Eaton that her brother was nothing but a gentleman that often came off as surly, Charlotte had worried that the man would be hard and cold. But he seemed nothing of the sort.

When he took her hand in his to help her up into the carriage, she felt his strength and warmth even through her glove. Her cheeks flushed as she smoothed her skirts to sit upon the board of the cart. When the sheriff sat down next to her, she gestured toward the horse that was pulling. "What a beautiful horse. Most of the horses that pull in Washington are dark colored like the ones for the stagecoach. This one almost shines like a gold coin."

The sheriff smiled. "His name is Nugget. I've had him for ten years now."

"He's quite handsome."

"I'm sure he likes hearing that," he said as he steered the cart, and the horse started a jaunty trot in front of them. "I think he's holding his head a little higher."

"Really?" Charlotte looked toward the horse in wonder if the horse might actually be holding himself differently or if the sheriff was just teasing her.

They were riding along for a little while when the sheriff took a deep breath and said, "I just wanted to let you know that we're going to wait a bit before the wedding. I don't want you to feel rushed into anything and we should make sure that we're getting along before we decide to tie the knot entirely."

Frowning, she nodded. His sister had warned that things could go either way. Mrs. Eaton had said that her brother wasn't one to rush into things and marriage was a big commitment for him. But once he was committed to something, her brother would give his all. On the other hand, she had warned, it was possible that she might be taken from stage-coach straight to the altar, since the marriage was one of convenience for him since he was running for public office. Regardless, Charlotte was unsure what to expect. "All right. I'm amenable to that."

"I'm glad to hear it," he said, his shoulders lowering a bit as he relaxed some. "I'm not sure how much my sister told you, but I'm not looking for a marriage in every way. I need a wife to create the image of roots and a family for the voters. But you can consider it a sort of partnership instead. I'm not looking for you to perform any normal wifely duties."

"Understood." She felt a bit flustered as he said it, but saw that his own discomfort was greater, as the tops of his ears turned quite pink. Taking the opportunity to study the sheriff's profile, Charlotte noted that he was quite a handsome man. His square jaw and angled features might have been considered severe by some, but there was a soft kindness to his eyes and mannerisms that assured her that he was a thoughtful gentleman and not at all lecherous or demanding like Mr. Montgomery. Her stomach soured at the thought of her former employer. In some ways it was wrong for her to compare that man with the man sitting next to her, but since she'd never courted with anyone, only her former boss had ever made an offer of marriage...even though it wasn't much of an offer as much as a means of manipulation. At least if she was to be a charm upon her husband's arm, Charlotte had a choice with the sheriff, and somehow she doubted that Mr. Montgomery would have made an offer of not expecting wifely duties as well.

After a half-hour of slow trotting down a road away from town, they pulled down a lane that led to a two-story house with three gables set overtop a covered porch. It was large and a long way from the nearest neighbor. That sort of scared her a little. As a resident of Georgetown in the city her whole life, she was used to having neighbors at hand at any time of need. What was she to do if she needed something? If it took half an hour for her to arrive by horse and cart, how long would the journey take her to walk? Over an hour for certain.

"My mother is awaiting us inside. I'm sure she's overjoyed to meet you." His face softened even more with a smile.

Uncertain whether he meant what he said, Charlotte lifted a brow. "Overjoyed?"

He pulled up the golden horse right in front of the house and then hopped down and came around quickly, offering her a hand to help her down from the seat. Then he nodded. "She's been pressuring me to get married for the past three years. Your arrival has been quite the godsend for her. I'm sure she could die happily now, especially since, as a seamstress, you're a kindred spirit."

Taking his offered hand, Charlotte frowned. "I hope that she lives a very long, healthy life, however."

He tilted his head at her. "Of course."

"My mother taught me to profess things as I want them to be—to always remember that God sees beyond what man sees. He sees things how they could and should be, and not necessarily as they are." Once she stood on her feet once more, she squeezed his fingers gently as a sign of affection before releasing them.

"So," the sheriff said, "If you declare things as they should or could be, you're agreeing with God."

A smile tugged at her lips. "That's exactly what I mean. And agreeing with God is a way of showing faith."

"Hmm." He offered her an elbow. "I've never quite thought of it that way before."

She took his arm and swallowed hard. Somehow, she'd gotten comfortable with the sheriff, but she was still nervous about meeting his mother. What if she was a hard woman who liked to nag? What if she wasn't as kind as her son and daughter? Those fears started to rise up but she pushed them down with what she knew to be true. How could a son and daughter as amicable as the sheriff and Mrs. Eaton have come from a home that was anything but loving and supportive? Yes, he mentioned that his mother nagged him about marriage, but he'd said it while smiling and in an almost joking way, which meant that he wasn't annoyed by her.

Reminding herself of these things, Charlotte took comfort and stepped toward the covered porch. Before they'd even made it to the steps, an older woman opened the front door, her smile and shining eyes almost exactly like Mrs. Eaton's. In fact, Mrs. Harris's daughter was the spitting image of her mother. She limped forward, favoring her left leg. "About time you made it back. I was afraid you'd dilly-dally the whole way home."

The sheriff stepped forward and took hold of his mother's elbow as he released Charlotte's hand. "Mother, you could have sat down and waited for us. I don't want you to hurt your ankle any more than you already have."

"Hodge-podge!" She yanked her elbow from his hand and waved dismissively. "This is nothing and I'll be back to walking straight in a day or two. Don't worry about it. I couldn't possibly just sit in a chair and wait for you all to come to me. I'm not a complete invalid, you know."

He sighed. "I know, mother."

"I needed to meet this young woman as soon as possible. It's amazing that your sister chose a bride for you so early. She is picky, you know. It may seem like she'd send you any old lady, but I know your sister. She wouldn't dare." That's when Mrs. Harris looked her up and down, her eyes appraising and then fixing on Charlotte's gaze again with an approving smile upon her lips. "You certainly are a pretty one. Did you have a profession before or were you from a family?"

"Mother! You shouldn't be so forward with your questions."

"Hush." She shook her head and glared at him. "When you get to be my age, you need to be honest and not beat around the bush." Then the older woman returned her softened gaze back to her. "Miss?"

"It's Miss Dunn—but please call me Charlotte." She looked between her and the sheriff. "Both of you."

The sheriff's mother straightened and smiled wider. "Of course, Charlotte. But I insist that you call me Mabel."

After clearing his throat, the sheriff said, "And please call me Simon, as well."

"All right," Charlotte said, nodding. "And to answer your other question, I was employed as a seamstress and dressmaker, I'd been working with Mr. Claude Montgomery for the last five years."

Mabel eyes widened in joy and surprise. "I was a seamstress also!"

Her smile was contagious, and Charlotte nearly laughed as she cast a glance toward Simon. "So, I've been told."

Then the older woman was looking over Charlotte's shoulder toward the cart. "Did you bring a sewing machine? I had to sell mine before making the move from Baltimore. I had the Singer Model 1. It was an old, but sturdy machine that I used for quite a few years before I had to stop because of my rheumatism," she said, holding up her hands and showing Charlotte her swollen joints.

"Oh," Charlotte said, "I'm sorry to hear that. Yes, I brought my machine with me. It's a Singer 11. Not the latest model, but it does me well."

Mabel's eyes sparkled. "I can't wait to see."

"All right, mother," Simon said as he started ushering his mother back toward the front door of the house. "That's enough. Let's all head inside. You can make Charlotte some tea, since I'm sure she's tired and thirsty from her journey. Maybe even hungry. I'll bring in her trunks—including the machine you're so desperate to see."

Mabel ducked under his arm and came back to Charlotte, looping arms with her. "I think we're going to be great friends, young lady. I'm so thrilled that you've come into our lives."

Charlotte's cheeks flushed at the older woman's praises. Although she'd always gotten along well with older ladies in church and in her neighborhood, she wasn't sure that was going to happen with her future mother-in-law. But her cheeks were beginning to ache from smiling so much. She allowed Mabel to lead her into the house and toward the kitchen.

CHAPTER 6

The next day, Simon eyed the sleeve on one of his work shirts. He was certain that it had a hole in it that he'd often get a finger stuck in when he'd pull his arm through it. Then, when he eyed where the hole should be, he found several tight stitches formed there in a color of thread that matched the pale blue of his shirt perfectly. Lifting a brow, he stepped over to his wardrobe and peered at his other shirt that had been missing a button on the bottom where he tucked it in. And as he'd imagined, the button had been replaced. He wandered into the kitchen still fingering the place where the hole had been. His mother sat at the kitchen table with a mug of coffee while Charlotte stood at the stove.

"Mother, did you mend my shirts?" He raised a brow at her.

"Of course not, dear. I just went into your wardrobe to get them and brought them to Charlotte so that she could show me how her machine works and get a couple things done to help you in the process."

"Do they sew buttons on with machines these days?"

Rolling her eyes, his mother shook her head. "Of course not, dear. She did that bit by hand. But she was able to show me some new techniques she's learned, and that newfangled machine is quite the wonder."

Then Charlotte turned around with a plate and set it down at the head of the table. She met eyes with him briefly, saying, "For you." And then turned back around and started on the next batch of pancakes.

"Hmm," he said, "Thank you."

And with that, he sat down in front of the plate. Charlotte may have had a pretty face, but it seemed that she wasn't much of a talker. Or maybe she didn't have as much personality as she seemed to before. What was worse was that Mother already seemed to be pulling the young lady in and making her into a puppet of sorts. Would Charlotte always do whatever his mother asked of her? Did she have no thoughts of her own? After pouring a little maple syrup over the cakes, he slowly cut off a bite. Not bad. The pancakes were light and fluffy and they soaked up the syrup well. Then he noticed that they tasted a little better than usual. He looked up at her. "What did you do differently to these? They don't quite taste the same as I'm used to."

She turned toward him, adjusting her apron a bit. "I'm not sure. Just the usual: eggs, flour, milk, baking powder, and butter."

"Butter?" Mother asked as Charlotte set a plate in front of her. "That's not a usual ingredient in the cakes I've made."

Charlotte shrugged her shoulders. "My mother was the one who taught me to make them that way. The cakes turn out a little richer and thicker if you add some melted butter to the batter."

After taking a bite, Mother nodded. "Your mother was right. The cakes are better this way. And you didn't add any sugar? Usually, I add a tablespoon of it to a batch to give it extra sweetness."

Shaking her head, Charlotte flipped the cakes she was currently cooking in the pan and turned back toward them, saying, "My mother always used to add two spoonfuls of sugar, but I accidentally forgot the sugar all together once when I was making the cakes, and felt that they turned out better. Besides, when you're adding maple syrup to them, they hardly need the extra sweetness on their own."

Mother nodded, and Simon had to agree. These were richer cakes that tasted a bit more savory than sweet, which actually somehow made them better. Maybe he'd been wrong about Charlotte, and she could think for herself a bit, at least when it came to cooking. "These are delicious. I quite like them. And thank you for mending my shirts, too."

She turned around finally with a third plate of cakes and set them at the empty chair just before having a seat, herself. Shyly, she looked over at him with a soft smile. "You're welcome."

And then she poured some syrup over her pancakes. They ate together in quiet for several moments and before long, Simon was the first to finish his plate, so he sat back, content, with his cup of coffee and peered over to the new lady in his home. "So, you worked as a seamstress in Washington. What made you decide to come all the way out here?"

After setting down her fork and wiping her

mouth with her napkin, she sat up a little straighter. "I felt that I needed to make a fresh start. My mother passed away last month..."

"Oh, no," Mother said with a worried brow. "I'm so sorry to hear that."

Charlotte looked down at her plate with her hands in her lap. "I miss her terribly, but it wasn't a surprise, either. She'd been battling health issues ever since she got influenza last winter. It was like she couldn't completely get over it. The cough and constant fevers wouldn't quite leave her. I... I hated to see her suffer for so long."

Mother reached across the table and set a hand on Charlotte's upper arm. "I imagine you did dear. You're doing well and staying strong. You took care of your mother, and I'm certain she's in a better place now."

"I believe it," Charlotte said, looking up with a sad smile and her eyes shining with unshed tears. "My mother knew the Lord and even though she couldn't attend church, she'd have me read from the Bible and pray with her every morning and evening, and every chance I could get. There was nothing she loved more than singing a good praise hymn."

"That's a blessing—a mother who loves the Lord. You can have peace that your mother is with Him."

"Yes. Thank you," Charlotte said, dabbing at the corners of her eyes with her napkin. Then she took a deep breath and continued, "I was finding it hard to go about normal life anymore without her. She was my only family, and it felt like, my only reason for living. I know that's not true, but that's how it felt when I was melancholy. And then my former employer... he..." She swallowed hard and looked as though she was trying to find the right words. "He behaved untoward and I could no longer work for him, so when I saw the advertisement for mail-order brides in Denver, I decided that perhaps it was time for a change of scenery."

Simon nodded and took another sip of his coffee. He couldn't imagine how sad his life would feel if he lost his mother and didn't have his sister nearby now. There were times when he thought he'd be happier if they had stayed back in Maryland, where he could imagine that they were doing well and that he didn't have to think and care for them more than sending back money to them when he could. Instead, having them with him assured him of their safety and security, and he could see and care for them himself. And although they both nagged him frequently, he understood that was their way of showing how they loved and worried for him. If they didn't care, they wouldn't bother with trying to help him all the time. And now he couldn't hardly imagine what life would be like if they weren't there. And if either or both of them were truly gone from this world and Simon was left alone, like it seemed Charlotte had been, he didn't know what he'd do. For a flickering moment, he could imagine the melancholy that Charlotte must have felt in her solitude. His heart hurt a little in his chest. "I hope that things will get better for you here."

Her gray eyes fixed upon his for a moment, and they softened. "Thank you," she said quietly.

Just a moment before, his heart was pricked, and with one look, she lightened it and made it squeeze in a whole different way. He cleared his throat to keep from coughing up the coffee he'd just sipped. Swallowing it, he added another sip to wash it all down and then he stood quickly, not wanting to deal with everything that he was feeling right now. "All right, ladies. I best get to work. I'll see you both this evening for supper."

"Don't work too hard," his mother said, always looking out for him.

"We'll have supper ready for you when you return," Charlotte said, as she stood with him. He eyed her for a moment, noticing that she wasn't quite finished yet with her breakfast, but she was standing with him, regardless.

It had been rude for him to get up while she was still eating, and he felt his stomach twist a bit at her own cordiality. "Thank you," he said, and then made a gesture for her to sit back down. "Please, continue your breakfast and don't mind me."

She nodded and then sat back down.

He grabbed his hat and strode to the back door. Once he stepped outside, he released a long breath and put his hat on his head before hopping down the steps. It was unusual for him to have company, but Charlotte was more than just company. They were to be getting to know each other and to be looking toward marriage. That made his stomach flip. Even though it was mainly full of dread, since marriage was the last thing he'd wanted to do, there was also something else present there now. Maybe if it was Charlotte, it wouldn't be so bad. She seemed quiet and kind and gentle. She didn't seek praise for mending his shirts, and allowed his mother to offer full explanation. Even after she'd given him his breakfast, she just quietly continued to work in the kitchen, not expecting anything for her work. This was different from what he'd expected. He frowned. What had he expected? He wasn't sure, but this definitely wasn't quite it. And Charlotte was the prettiest thing he'd seen in quite some time. She outshined everyone in town, and even back when he was young and in Maryland, he couldn't quite remember ever seeing anyone so pretty.

Nugget nickered at him as he entered the barn, and a thought flashed through his mind. Charlotte was even prettier and kinder than Sarah. Frowning he took hold of his saddle and entered the stall to tack up his gelding. Why did he think such a thing? It was unfair to Charlotte to compare her to his first love like that. After placing the saddle on Nugget's back, he reached under his belly to take hold of the cinch. Honestly, somewhere along the way, he'd convinced himself that all women were basically the same. That they would all break his heart and cause him to feel the pain of being alone eventually. That they couldn't be trusted with his heart, because they could turn their back on him at any time. He huffed out a long breath as he finished knotting the cinch to the saddle. Then he reached for his bridle.

Maybe he was wrong to think that way. Maybe he shouldn't have believed that for as long a time as he did. Maybe Charlotte was different. But maybe not.

Once he pulled the bridle over Nugget's ears, he

went to tie the throat latch and stopped a moment, staring at the leather in the shadowed light of the small barn. He didn't need to tie it anymore, because the buckle had been repaired. How? When had a new buckle been sewn onto the leather? He'd driven Nugget to town yesterday with his harness and cart bridle, leaving his riding bridle behind. Had his mother given his bridle for Charlotte to repair, too? After buckling the bridle, he looked up at the house. This new bride of his was a strange one. How was he to respond to this? She cooked, she helped his mother, and she was sewing and helping him as well. Did she feel that she needed to earn her keep? Did she think that doing these little repairs and such that it was some way of paying them back? She didn't need to do such a thing.

Simon opened the door to the stall and led Nugget out of the barn. Then he mounted smoothly and started for the road. Part of him wanted to go back in the house and say something to Charlotte about these things, but the other part of him knew he had things to do, and there'd be no real purpose in talking to her about these things now. He frowned as he found a cart approaching him about a mile up past his house. When the cart pulled closer, he found Mrs. Francis at the reins. He pulled up as she stopped the cart.

"Good morning," he called over to her.

"Good morning," she answered in a sing-song voice. "I've come to call on this new bride of yours— to give her a proper welcome to the town and such."

Simon nodded. He knew that this was likely to be coming. "I'm sure Charlotte and my mother will both be happy for the company."

With a gesture toward the road she said, "Well, I don't know why you need to live all the way out this way from town. It's nearly three miles!"

He shrugged. "It's not too far. Only takes me a few minutes to get to town on horseback."

"Well, if there were an emergency of some kind, it might not be a bad idea to have the sheriff a bit closer. I mean... look what happened in Castle Rock just yesterday."

"Castle Rock?" He frowned. "What happened?"

"Oh," she said, her eyebrows lifting. "I suppose you might not have heard yet, since it all only happened in the evening, and I was only privy to it because Mr. Francis was at a cattleman's meeting in Castle Rock. Well anyway, Mr. Holt—you remember Jeb Holt, don't you—well he thwarted a robbery attempt at the bank just as it was closing. Caught two of the robbers with the help of his cattle hands. Can you believe it? Then when he sent the hands to bring the robbers to the jailhouse here in Franktown, the hands were ambushed in the dark by more of those outlaws and the robbers got away."

He blinked at her. "Were the cowhands injured?"

She shook her head. "Apparently, they were held at gunpoint and were grossly outnumbered, so they did as the outlaws said. Their cooperation likely saved their lives."

"I imagine so," Simon said as he thought about what this all meant. He nodded toward her. "Thank you for letting me know, but I best be getting to town and dealing with all of this."

She nodded toward him. "I'll be seeing you later, sheriff."

After reining Nugget toward town, he galloped off, determined to make it there quickly to find out what had been going on. If these robbers were part of that same rash of robberies that had been hitting counties surrounding Denver, their county was likely to be next. If a robbery was thwarted, but no one officially arrested, it might mean that the outlaws would try again soon. He needed to question all the witnesses involved so that he could find out where these men were. And then, if Crowley was right, and the ringleader was someone local to the area, it would have been great to have had robbers to question. Still, he'd have to make do with what he had. He pulled to a stop in front of the livery and hopped off Nugget quickly. He handed the reins over to the livery man. "Don't put him out in the paddock just yet, Sam. I might need to head to Castle Rock right away."

Sam, the livery owner, nodded. "Yes sir."

Unsure what was his best move right now, Simon headed toward the sheriff's office to find out what he could there first.

CHAPTER 7

Charlotte poured Mrs. Francis a cup of tea and then set out the cookies that Mabel had showed her were in a tin for just such occasions. The new lady's eyes were watching Charlotte, and she could feel them on her as she moved to pour a cup for Mabel as well.

"You certainly are a pretty one," Mrs. Francis said as she took a lump of sugar and stirred it into her tea. "I didn't know they made mail-order brides so pretty. I figured that your kind wouldn't have much of a struggle finding a husband wherever you were, and the plain ones would be those that might end up on a train out here to the west."

"I suppose that my son got lucky there, then," Mabel said with the slightest edge to her voice.

Charlotte hadn't even known the elder woman very long, but she could tell the irritation was there.

Mrs. Francis, however, didn't seem to notice or didn't seem to mind, for she continued assessing Charlotte as though she were cattle for sale instead of a lady in the same room. "Her mannerisms are graceful, too. But I can't help but think that she must be a little dull if she needed to come all this way to find good marriage prospects."

Charlotte stopped in her tracks, a little bit of anger rising up in her, and she gripped the handle of the teapot she was about to set back on the stove. She held her breath so that she wouldn't say something untoward to a complete stranger and end up upsetting her potential future family.

But, Mabel cleared her throat. "Not at all. Miss Dunn is quite the enterprising youth. I'll have you know that she is a seamstress and dressmaker who has designed some of the latest and greatest fashions that have been going around in the highest social circles of Washington DC over the last few years."

Able to breathe again, Charlotte set the pot down upon the stovetop and turned around to Mrs. Francis's gaze appraising her anew, eyebrows raised. "Really? Is that so? Do you have your own sewing machine then?"

Fighting a frown, Charlotte nodded. "Yes, Mrs. Francis."

A smile lit up the woman's face and suddenly she looked ten years younger and much less severe than she had been a moment before. "That's wonderful news. Just wonderful. Franktown has been in need of a dressmaker for years and years. Everyone has to head to Denver to get the latest in fashion trends and to get even the simplest of dresses made." She gestured toward Charlotte with open hands. "But now we have our very own dressmaker and fashion insight arrived in Franktown. Could you imagine if ladies from Denver even came to have dresses made in our county? That would be an amazing feat. You must make a dress for me. I insist. We have a ball and joint party on Christmas Eve for the Cattleman's Association and the Temperance League each year. Could you make me a dress for the event? It's six weeks away... that's enough time, isn't it?"

Charlotte could no longer fight her frown as she thought about making the dress. "I... I don't have the materials or fabric to make the dress."

"There's a haberdasher in town and he often gets the latest fabrics from Denver. I buy things there all the time and try to make things with my own, minimal sewing talent, but to have a real and true dressmaker here? I cannot wait to see what you can do. I'm so excited."

Even though the lady had been on the verge of mean only a few minutes before, her excitement and joy at the prospect of a new dress was catching. Charlotte's imagination was already swirling with ideas for possible designs and colors, and she couldn't wait to get her hands on some fabrics. "I'll need to take measurements and know what kinds of ideas you have for colors and how many layers of fabric you'd want. But it should take me less than a week to finish a dress for you once I have materials."

Mrs. Francis's eyes sparkled. "Less than a week! That is amazing. Once the Temperance League hears about this, I'm certain you'll get more ladies who will want dresses before the ball as well. You might have a very busy couple of weeks between now and Christmas." Then the lady's eyes looked back and forth between the two of them. "You should both come to the bridge club meeting tonight, since several of the ladies will be there. Do you play?"

Charlotte blinked and met gazes with Mabel for a moment. Mabel nodded to her with a soft smile, so Charlotte decided to nod as well. "I know the game, but don't play well."

"That's quite all right," Mrs. Francis said with a grin. "There are several ladies in the club that don't play very well, either, but we don't hold it against them." She huffed a laugh at her own joke. "Anyway, I usually pay about thirty-five dollars for a dress that I get made in Denver for the party. Would that be enough for you to get the fabric you need and pay you for your time?"

One thing that she'd learned from Mr. Montgomery was to school her expression in these situations since she didn't know for sure if acting too elated about the price would make the lady have second thoughts about what she was paying. Mr. Montgomery was not a good man, but he was right in what he would say about how people didn't appreciate what they don't pay for. If they get things too cheaply, they tend to treat it as though it was unimportant or cheap. But if something was expensive, they tended to treat it better simply because of the price that they paid. In her limited experience, Charlotte saw these scenarios both play out. And with the kind of money that Mrs. Francis was talking, if she could make six or eight dresses for the event, she could pay a large amount toward the debt that she owed her neighbors. Even though she knew that Mr. Montgomery would charge more than double what Mrs. Francis had offered, it was kind of her to offer that much without truly seeing yet what kind of dress Charlotte could even make for her. "Yes, I can do that for thirty-five dollars. I'll need to get to the haberdasher tomorrow in order to see what fabrics and such are available." She turned her gaze toward Mabel. "Do you think that would be possible?"

Mabel nodded, her smile widening. "I believe so."

"Very good," Mrs. Francis said as she stood. "Let's get started with those measurements then?"

SIMON RODE OUT TO CASTLE ROCK AFTER HEARING what he could from Mr. Francis about the robbery that had happened the day before. Unfortunately, word was already going around that Jeb Holt might be throwing his hat in the ring to become the sheriff of Douglas County, and catching the robbers was just proof that he might be qualified to do so. Once Simon pulled in front of the bank in Castle Rock, he dismounted and tied Nugget to the hitching post. Then he stepped inside the building. It was just past nine o'clock, so the bank had only been open for a few minutes. No other patrons were in the bank, which had red ribbons and bows of holly already decorating the walls in celebration of the upcoming holiday. After removing his hat, Simon headed toward the teller. "Is the manager in? It's Sheriff Harris."

The teller's eyes went a little wide and he nodded. "Yes, sir. He's expecting you. In the office to the right."

Simon followed the man's gesture and strode over to the office. The door was open, but Simon still knocked before stepping in. At the desk sat a man with thinning gray hair who looked up and over the spectacles he wore at the sound of Simon's knock. Without saying a word, the man gestured toward the chair across from his desk and then continued writing in the ledger he'd been working in when Simon had knocked.

Not long after Simon sat down, the banker closed the ledger and removed his spectacles. He rubbed the red marks on both sides of his nose. "Sheriff Harris, I've been expecting you."

"Yes, sir." Simon leaned forward, his hat still in his hands. "Could you tell me about what happened yesterday?"

The gentleman frowned. "I had heard about the

rash of robberies that have been happening around Denver, but mainly to the west and north, but we all assumed it was a matter of time before the robbers came to the south. Due to this, I'd increased the number of my security guards from one to three, but yesterday, two of those guards did not make it in. One of them had given me word the day before that he was not feeling well, so it was not unexpected. Now we've since found out that the other guard had gone missing and is still missing to this point. This makes us wonder if the robbers might have had something to do with that as well."

"Then there is a missing person as well as the robbery to report."

The man shrugged a bit. "To some extent. It wasn't much of a robbery since soon after the robbers came in and threatened the teller at gunpoint, Mr. Jeb Holt and three of his cowboys entered and they drew guns on the robbers. Since there were only two robbers and four of them, it was a smart move for them to lay down their weapons instead of their lives."

"So, that's how things went?"

"Jeb Holt had his men tie up the outlaws and kept the bank from losing a single dime that day. Then, even though it was dusk, those three cowboys went down to deliver the robbers to your office, but apparently were ambushed along the way by ten more outlaws. Then, again, the smartest plan of action was to lay down weapons and give the outlaws their way in order to keep from losing lives."

"Then, as far as the robbery was concerned, no lives were taken."

"Unless, that is, Mr. Frank Smith, the missing security guard has lost his life in some nefarious way. Mr. Smith is a widower in town and has been guarding the bank here for coming up on fifteen years. He's never missed a day of work."

"Then Mr. Smith was the guard that you already had in your employ before hiring two new ones?"

"Yes, sheriff. That's correct."

"All three guards worked every day?"

"Yes. We are closed on Saturday and Sunday, so the guards...and all of the employees work each and every day that we are open."

"Are the two guards in today?"

"They are. And we've already hired a third one to replace Frank Smith, temporarily."

"All right." Simon stood from his chair. "I'll need to get the address of Mr. Frank Smith and also Mr. Jeb Holt. I'll need to question both of them on this."

As the banker stood, a slight frown tugged at his

lip. "I'm happy to give you the address of Mr. Smith, but Mr. Holt is out of town. He had stopped into the bank to make a withdrawal. According to him, he's headed up to the auction house in Denver today for the 4 p.m. livestock sale. But he left word that he'd meet you in Franktown tomorrow."

"I see. I'll look into the missing Mr. Frank Smith then."

"Sounds good," the banker said as he replaced his spectacles in order to scribble something quickly on a piece of paper. "Here's where you will find Mr. Smith."

Simon headed out the door and mounted Nugget once he was outside. Mr. Smith lived on the west end of the small village of Castle Rock, in a room above his son's butcher's shop. When Simon arrived, he found the butcher at work with a cleaver in hand, taking apart a leg quarter. The man looked up when the bell above the door rang and squinted at Simon. "Can I help you?"

Simon removed his hat. "I'm the sheriff. I was wondering if you know where I might find your father?"

The man shook his head, his brow still creased as he frowned. "I already checked upstairs, but my father's bed doesn't even look like it's been slept in."

"Is your father prone to disappearing like this? Does he have another place where he might rest his head?"

The butcher shook his head. "My father does nothing differently at all. Every day he does the same thing—you could set your clock by him. So, it's terribly unusual for him to not be home at night."

Simon looked about the room. "Does he help you at all here in the butcher shop? Isn't this usually a family-learned occupation?"

The man nodded. "Yes, but it wasn't my father's shop. My father-in-law only had the one child, and she is Luella, the woman I married. When I did, I learned the trade and eventually took over the shop."

"I see. And your father then moved into the rooms upstairs?"

"Yes sir."

"Would you allow me to look around at the rooms?"

"Help yourself, sheriff. The stairs are in the back." Then the man turned his attention back to the leg quarter.

Simon walked around the counter and headed for the stairs. Once at the top of the stairs, he looked about at the small apartment that consisted of a bedroom, a kitchen, and a living area where the kitchen table sat halfway into since the kitchen itself was just a few cabinets along the wall with a wood stove sitting on bricks. A mug of half-drank coffee sat upon the kitchen table, the blackness within already forming into a sludge, and when Simon picked up the cup, it sloshed a bit, allowing him to see the ring forming where the coffee had been sitting. When he stepped over to the stove, he found that the wood within were ashes. It hadn't been put out but rather burned down entirely. When Simon peered into the bedroom, he found the bed made and unslept in. There were no clothes lying around, but he did notice the pair of boots that sat at the edge of the stairs. Probably the only boots that Mr. Smith had.

So, it seemed unlikely that Mr. Smith had left the loft while barefoot. If it was the morning of the robbery, that day had been a bit chilly, with a touch of frost upon the ground. No one would have been caught out there barefoot. He stepped down a couple of steps to see if there was any evidence that the man had been taken on the stairs, but he couldn't see any traces of anything untoward. Then when he turned back, he noticed a scrape in the hardwood floor from where the chair had likely been dragged with weight in it.

Frowning, he headed back down the steps to the butcher who was already wrapping the meat he'd just chopped in paper. Clearing his throat, Simon asked, "You said that you went up to look for your father when the banker was looking for him, right? When was that?"

"Last night. I had already closed up the shop and was getting ready to head home. Mr. Harvey, the banker, came over and asked about my dad. I went upstairs to fetch him but didn't find him there."

"Did you pick anything up? Make the bed? Or change anything at all from the way that you found it?"

Slowly the man shook his head and then he stopped. "The kitchen chair was knocked over and I picked it up and set it upright, but other than that, I don't think I changed anything else."

It was just as Simon had figured. "All right. Did your father have any friends or go anywhere that I might ask about him?"

"He had no friends—he's an older man who used to work in the mines up in Idaho Springs back in the day, but now all his compatriots are long gone. I went around to the shops in town and to the saloon, and no one's seen hide nor hair of him." The butcher's brow creased. "Do you think something might have happened to my father?"

"It's beginning to seem like it."

The butcher's frown deepened, and there was a strained sadness about his eyes. "If it's these outlaws, will you do what you can to catch them?"

Simon rotated his hat in his hands. "I'll do everything I can to do just that. And if your father's all right, I do my best to find him as well."

"Thank you."

A little thought came to his mind. Why hadn't this man expressed support for Jeb Holt the way that the others did, since he'd been the one to catch some of these criminals in the act. Simon wanted to ask but decided to go indirectly instead. "I'm going to be questioning Jeb Holt tomorrow, is there anything you think I should ask him?"

The man's frown remained unchanged as he shook his head. "I wouldn't rightly know. But I don't really trust the man."

Simon lifted a brow. "Really? Why is that?"

"He's not the most honest when it comes to dealing with me. He's been the kind to try to overestimate a steer's weight and to try to get me to pay just a few more cents per pound as well. He even pulled one over on my wife when I had her running the register, saying that I had told him three cents per pound instead of two. It's just the little things, but if a man can't be honest with little things, will he have integrity with big ones?"

Simon furrowed his brow. "Do other people in Castle Rock feel that way?"

"I guess it depends on who you talk to. Mr. Holt is well liked for the most part." Then the butcher gestured toward Simon's star. "He says he's going for the office of sheriff. I hope that you beat him... You have my vote."

"Thank you," Simon said as he backed up a step toward the door. "You've been very helpful, and I will do everything I can to help your father. Let's all pray he's still alive."

"I will be doing just that, sir."

"Me too."

And with that, Simon stepped back outside and replaced his hat. He peered around the sleepy little town of Castle Rock. Even if Jeb Holt was a dishonest man when it came to pennies and cattle, he'd stopped a robbery in progress and attempted to turn in the criminals who'd perpetrated the crime. He still managed to do well by the voters in Douglas County, and Simon was sure that word would get out about it. Still, maybe the butcher was right. Maybe a man who couldn't be honest about the little things couldn't be trusted with big ones. And maybe that was just the reason that Simon needed to make sure that Mr. Holt didn't take office as sheriff. If he let little things slide as sheriff, they could easily turn into big ones. After untying Nugget, Simon swung himself into the saddle and started the ride home.

CHAPTER 8

That evening after supper, Simon decided that he really needed to get to know his future wife a little better, if that was the direction that they were going. He was still uncertain about that and didn't know yet if he even wanted to get married solely for the purpose of the election, only to lose the election anyway, and then be stuck with a woman who didn't want to be married to him, either. And then there was the rumor that he couldn't get better than a mail-order bride anyway. Maybe that rumor was true, but it still stung a bit. So, Simon asked Charlotte if she'd take a walk with him while he finished up his evening chores.

She nodded, and the two of them stepped out into the chilly evening just before sunset. Charlotte pulled her shawl a little tighter to her shoulders. "Does it always get this cold in November?"

"Unfortunately, it's usually worse than this. So far, we've been having a rather mild transition from autumn into winter."

"I see," she said, as he took her hand and helped her down the steps of the porch. "Georgetown doesn't seem to get quite this cold for at least another month."

"I believe it. I'm not sure that we told you that we're originally from Maryland—Baltimore, actually. So, we weren't too far from where you're from either."

"That's true. I forget that you all haven't lived too long here in Colorado, either."

He shrugged. "A little over ten years now, for me."

"And before that you served in the war?" she asked as they reached the barn, and Simon pushed the door open wide.

Nugget nickered to them as they stepped inside. "If you'd like to get a scoop of oats and put it in that pan next to the bag of feed, I'll fill up his water."

Charlotte nodded and did as he asked while Simon began pumping the well spigot that led directly to the trough in front of all the stalls. Nugget had a back door to his stall that led directly to the four-acre paddock that he shared with the milking cow and her calf. Those were the only two larger animals that they had in addition to the eight hens they had in the coop. It was enough to give them fresh milk and eggs and travel to and from Franktown.

The last question that she'd asked still niggled at his brain. He didn't much like to think of that time in his life, but he supposed that she deserved to know everything, if she was going to become his wife. "I got training in the Calvary and as a sharpshooter in the war, but I didn't see much in the way of battle. I only joined when there was a year and a half left in the war, and by then, the worst battles were over. The south had all but lost and only needed to surrender. Still it was a way to get away from home after my father died. He sort of left us all in shambles. I sent the little bit of money that I got for being in the army back to my mother and sister. And when I returned home from the war, I found my mother was making a reasonable enough living, scraping by as a seamstress and dressmaker."

"I see." Charlotte nodded as she gave Nugget the feed pan. The water trough was filled, so Simon stopped pumping and let the last bit of water run from the faucet and into the trough before tying it down again.

"Soon after, I left to head out west to make my fortune, found my calling as a lawman, and then I sent money back to support my family until they made their way out here to me, only three years ago." Simon let out a soft sigh as he looked into the shadows around the barn. Family was the most important thing, and a sadness came over him as he thought about the butcher, the younger Mr. Smith, who was now mourning the loss of his father, whose body they had found just before Simon had left Castle Rock. Without question there was foul play involved, since he was found by the river and was barefoot.

Charlotte's giggle brought him back to the present. She petted Nugget on the nose and then scratched his forehead as he ate his oats. "Are you sure you have the time to take me to town tomorrow?"

He nodded. "It'll be fine. I'm just going in a bit early, so you may have to find a way to occupy yourself while waiting for the haberdashery to open. And I'm not sure exactly what time I'll be available to take you back home, but I'll do my best not to keep you waiting for too long."

"That's kind of you," she said, a smile spreading across her lips as Nugget picked up his head and leaned into her scratches. "Apparently his face was itchy."

"Apparently," Simon said as he watched his ornery gelding show affection toward this woman that he didn't know. At best, Nugget usually showed indifference toward strangers, otherwise, he might give them a bit of a grumpy face. But with Charlotte, he seemed to take an instant liking. But come to think of it, Nugget hadn't spent much time around those of the female persuasion to begin with. Was that the difference?

"Is there any particular kind of snack that Nugget likes?" she asked.

Simon shrugged. "Apples and carrots, I suppose. Most horses have a liking toward those."

"And some like lump sugar, too, I understand."

"They do," Simon said as he reached over and patted the horse on the forehead. Nugget went back to eating his oats and swished his tail toward Simon as though the gelding was irritated with him. That was the Nugget that he knew.

"I suppose when we go to town in the morning, I'll need to pick up some extra apples or carrots for him. Whichever they happen to have right now."

"I imagine that they will have both, since it's autumn."

"I could get enough to make apple butter and some for cider as it gets cooler."

Simon quirked a brow. "I haven't had a good apple butter in a decade."

Her eyes went wide as she turned toward him. "You haven't?"

He shook his head. "I didn't even ask my mother if she had a recipe for it. I plum forgot about apple butter all together until you just suggested it, and now I've got a hankering for it."

Laughter shook her. "Well, sir, making apple butter happens to be one of my specialities."

"Shirt mending and bridle mending and now apple butter," he said while shaking his head. "Who knew that a mail-order bride could be so handy to have around?"

She waved a hand at him, her giggles still bubbling up. It was good to see her smiling and laughing. When she did this, it made him feel lighter and somehow happier, too. If he could make her smile and laugh like this all the time, it almost felt like he wouldn't mind having a wife around like her. His affection for her was already starting to grow into a friendship, and it was surprising to think that she'd only arrived the day before.

When they returned to the house, he was already feeling much better about this moment that they'd taken in order to get to know each other better. He hoped for many more situations like this and that they might make it a habit for her to come out and help him do the evening chores in the barn so that they could.

THE NEXT MORNING, CHARLOTTE SAT ON THE WOODEN bench on the front of the cart, holding hands with Mabel who sat between her and the sheriff as they made their way to town. A fog still settled on the land, making the morning sunlight seem golden and coming from all directions. Charlotte's breath fogged around her face before it was torn away by the wind created by their traveling cart. Once they arrived in front of the livery, Simon gave each of them a hand in getting down and then left them to their own devices while he took care of Nugget and the cart there.

Mabel walked beside her, and it soothed Charlotte that Mabel seemed to be walking without a limp anymore. It had been a trouble spot for Simon that his mother insisted on continuing to do things instead of resting and healing her injury, no matter how small it might be. When they made their way to the mercer and haberdashery to see what time it would open, the gentleman within spotted them and came directly to the door. "Hello, ladies. It's a fine morning. What brings you both by?"

Mabel had her arm looped with Charlotte's, and she gave it a squeeze as she said to the man, "My son's fiancé, here is in need of fabric. She's a fine dressmaker and has just been commissioned to make a dress for Mrs. Francis, the leader of the Temperance League."

His eyes sparkled. "A dressmaker! Why, that's just what Franktown has needed for quite a while. No more need for ladies of fashion to head to Denver for their dresses if we have a fine dressmaker here in town." He opened the door wider for them and gestured for them to come inside. "We don't normally open for another quarter hour, but how could I possibly make you two ladies continue to stand out in this horrid chill."

Once inside, she and Mabel marveled over the fine selection of fabrics that they had. Keeping in mind that Mrs. Francis preferred a green dress,

Charlotte chose two different greens made of different materials so that they could complement each other when layered together. With all of this, she could make the dress that she'd sketched quickly for Mrs. Francis the afternoon before. It excited Charlotte as she went through the reds and whites too. As she hoped that she might be able to get more fabrics for more dresses, she went through as many of the bolts as possible.

"If you have more left over from Mrs. Francis's up-front payment, perhaps you should look into getting extra fabrics, and start working on another dress or two. Even if you don't sell them right away, you'd have stuff for the window of your storefront when you get a shop in town."

Charlotte froze and turned toward Mabel. "A shop in town?"

Mabel nodded as she fingered a bit of satin fabric. "Why not? You've heard what everyone has said. We need a dressmaker in Franktown. It's a blessing that you've come all the way here."

A blessing? Charlotte knew that God's hand was at work in her life, but sometimes it took getting past a situation before she could see where His handiwork had been. Ever since she'd arrived in Franktown, two days ago, she'd heard several times that a dressmaker was exactly what the town had need of. And now she'd arrived. What if she'd gone somewhere different, where they'd already had three dressmakers, then Charlotte might have had to be content with making clothing for her own children alone. Though there was a certain amount of desirability in that prospect, the prospect of having her own store in town was one that she'd never even dared to imagine until that moment.

"If you're looking for a certain color, pattern, or material, let me know right away. I'm Drake by the way," he said as he gestured toward the front door and the words painted there, and said them aloud, "Gregor Drake, Haberdasher and Mercer."

"It's lovely to meet you finally," said Mabel. "I'm Mabel Harris, the sheriff's mother."

Then they both looked expectantly at her. Charlotte bowed slightly. "Charlotte Dunn, dressmaker and..." she paused to take a breath and steel herself before saying, "the future Mrs. Harris."

A wide smile spread across both of their faces at her introduction. Mr. Drake said, "We're all happy to see that the sheriff is settling down here in Franktown. Even though he's been a deputy for quite a few years, it's different when you have family here too."

Then he turned to Mabel. "And that includes you, too."

"Well, thank you," Mabel said as she preened.

For several minutes, they looked at all the different fabrics, and Charlotte chose enough to make two more dresses, as Mabel had suggested. Each of the dresses that she had planned in her mind would be good for wearing to the Christmas Eve Ball, and if no one liked them, she could use them as Mabel had suggested. Then her fingers found a bit of white lace and a wedding dress formed in her mind. Heat rose to her cheeks as she thought about wearing it herself as she walked down the aisle, and at the end of it, stood Sheriff Simon Harris.

Immediately she let go of the lace and cleared her throat, peering at Mabel and hoping that no one had noticed the color that had reached her cheeks. She was getting far too ahead of herself. Yes, Simon was a handsome man. He seemed caring and kind, and together they'd begun developing a friendship, but was it love? She wasn't sure. No matter what they'd been saying to one another while spending time together, she couldn't help but feel as though the sheriff was holding back. It was understandable, since she was a stranger and they didn't know each other very well, but something inside her hoped that they could get past that small problem, whatever it might be, and perhaps wed and become the family that she'd imagined having.

Letting out a slow breath, she shook those thoughts from her head. Again, she was getting ahead of herself, and she needed to keep God in control of her life, and not try to take control herself. Then she stepped up to the counter with the bolts of fabric that she wanted and allowed the haberdasher to cut them to the lengths that she desired. Afterward, she paid the man, and felt good about her purchases as they stepped back out of the shop and into the street. They went a few buildings down and stopped in the general store to pick up apples and a bag of flour. Mabel had been excited at the prospect of learning Charlotte's apple butter recipe.

After they came out of the general store, Mabel took hold of her arm lightly. "Why don't you go ahead and find Simon to let him know we're ready to go? That way if we have a bit of a wait, it's not too long. And I'll just head inside the millinery for a moment to have a word with the hat maker."

"Oh, I'll go with you."

She waved a hand in dismissal. "No need. I'll be fine. Just go find Simon."

Charlotte eyed the older woman for a moment and watched her head into the hat shop. It really wouldn't have been much for Charlotte to go with Mabel and for them to do all these things together, but for some reason, Mabel wanted to separate herself. Perhaps it was because the older woman wanted to offer up time for Charlotte to be alone with Simon for a few moments without her constant interference as chaperone. In so doing, it was likely that Charlotte and Simon would grow closer together. And in that way, she supposed that his mother was right. With a deep breath, she steeled herself and started in the direction of the sheriff's office.

When she was just a little bit away, the door to the office opened and out stepped a bigger, rough-looking older man with a long mustache to go with his dark hair, which was immediately covered with a gray felt hat. Following him was the sheriff, a little bit of a frown on his face marring his usually soft and handsome features. Simon said, "Thank you for coming in, Mr. Holt."

"I'm sorry I couldn't be of more use to you. I didn't really get a good look at those men, but they didn't seem recognizable to me. Likely out-of-town-ers, I'd say."

"Right," Simon said, his brow creasing a bit further, then his eyes shot in her direction and his glare softened a little bit.

Following his gaze, the bigger man, Mr. Holt, turned toward Charlotte as well, and his brow immediately rose as a sneer joined his features. "Ah, is this your mail-order bride that I'd heard about? She really is as pretty as people have been saying. But still, it makes me wonder what must be wrong with her to be desperate enough to answer the call to come out west. What kind of checkered past must she have?" he asked with a chuckle.

Charlotte's heart dropped toward her stomach and felt cold. Was that what people were thinking and saying of her?

But Simon's gaze sharpened and a fire blazed behind his eyes. "That's enough of speculation and gossip. I'll have you know that my bride-to-be has a heart for helping others and a gift for her work that has already enriched our community. To paint her decision to move West with no knowledge of the facts is reckless and unfair. It is not the time for you to sling mud in an election campaign and to use her as fodder. If you take issue with me, that's one thing, but I won't stand idly by while you attack an innocent woman's reputation. Charlotte is a person of integrity and substance, and I'm honored she chose our town as her new home. You owe her an apology for your unfair mischaracterization."

"Hmph," the man said with his hands on his hips, then turned his glare upon Charlotte, though it had more reluctance in it than anger or hatred. He tipped his hat. "Excuse my assumptions, Miss. I only meant them in jest."

Charlotte had a hand upon her heart, but she said nothing, nor gestured to respond to the man's half-hearted apology. But it made no difference; his gaze slipped past her as the man turned and strode toward a group of three other men who'd been standing by the hitching post a few yards away. One of them handed him the reins of a sorrel horse and he mounted quickly. The other three followed suit and without so much as a glance backward, they all rode off to the north.

"I'm sorry that you had to be subject to that, Charlotte," Simon's kind voice signified that he'd stepped closer while her gaze was distracted.

She shook her head. "It's quite all right. You cannot control other people's thoughts or what they might say." Still, something ached inside her chest at what the man had said. What if others in town felt the same way. She knew that she shouldn't care much about what other people thought, since it was God who knew the truth and knew her heart, but she'd hate it if she was the cause of the sheriff to lose some of his own reputation because he took defense of her. However, the other part of her was very happy that Simon had defended her honor, because it had showed that wasn't the way he felt about her, and that much was a great relief. Slowly, she let out a breath, and then allowed a smile to tug at her lip. "Your mother sent me to fetch you since we're finished with our shopping."

Immediately the wrinkles between Simon's brows softened and a small smile played on his lips. "Oh? So soon? Did you find everything that you needed?"

She nodded, the pinprick of worry taking flight as the excitement of new fabrics and making the dresses she had in her head filled her instead. "We did. I believe that Mrs. Francis will be quite pleased with the dress I intend to make for her."

"I'm certain she will be. My mother says you have quite the talent, and she doesn't just go around dishing out those kind of compliments about things such as dressmaking. She's usually quite particular."

"I am," Mabel said as she arrived behind Charlotte. "And my son tells the truth there, you do have quite the talent, and I can't wait to see what you come up with for changing the fashion in our little town. I'm certain that your good reputation will be bringing ladies from Denver to Franktown to buy the latest in your designs."

Charlotte's heart soared a bit. "I only hope that I have half the success that you imagine for me."

"Humility is a great thing, but don't doubt yourself and your own abilities." Mabel squeezed her arm. "It's all right to acknowledge and utilize your talents. Don't forget, even Jesus admonished the servant who buried his talent in the ground instead of nurturing it and allowing it to multiply."

Smiling, Charlotte nodded her thanks. Her mother had always said that she'd had a talent for sewing and making dresses, but mothers were always supposed to support their daughters, so she'd not thought too much of it. Mr. Montgomery used to praise her talents in the beginning, but as time went on, he tended to criticize her works more often instead. To have someone who was known for her talent with the needle, like Mabel, and who didn't have to be so kind, praise Charlotte's work made her happy. "Well, we'll see if my dresses live up to your standards once they are made."

"I'm certain they will."

"Well," Simon said, "I'm finished for the morning here, so I'll take you both home and get a quick bite to eat before returning if that will suit you?"

"It will," Mabel and Charlotte said at the same time. Then they met eyes with each other and shared a small laugh. It felt good for Charlotte to have an encouraging woman in her life again, and being with Mabel was healing that part of her, but she couldn't help but wish that her mother could have been as healthy into her older age like this too. She sighed wistfully as they headed for the livery to fetch Nugget and the cart.

CHAPTER 9

A little over two weeks went past, and Charlotte had gotten into a routine with the sheriff and his mother. They spent their breakfasts together, Charlotte then helped Mabel with chores to keep up the house and laundry, then she spent hours sewing and working on the dresses for the Christmas ball, and in the evenings Simon returned for dinner and afterward, chores in the barn. Of late, those chores in the barn seemed to be taking longer than before. As the two of them got to know each other, Charlotte found that she was loathe to end their conversations.

"Do you know why an apple is better than a pear?" Simon asked with a smile.

Unsure if it was a joke that he was telling this time, or telling her his preference, she shrugged. "I'm afraid I don't know."

"Apples have variety. Some are very sweet, some are a little bit sour. Some are green while others are red. Then you have the mushy kind while others are quite crunchy. It makes them a little bit unpredictable, so that if someone says that they have apples, you're never quite sure what kind of apple you're going to get until you see and taste."

She lifted a brow. "And pears?"

"Always the same color and always the same gritty mealiness. It's also the reason I don't much care for grits."

A laugh escaped her. "I suppose that Mason-Dixon Line delineating the north from the south is quite right then, since you are disrespecting the common southern breakfast."

He leaned back against the wood of the stall where the milk cow and calf would spend their time in inclement weather, while sitting on a bale of straw. "I suppose they did. Maryland has some southern roots and charm, but we're definitely north in spirit."

Between her own fingers, a piece of straw spun,

it's gold reflecting in the light of the lantern. Even though it was a little chilly out, the inside of the barn and sitting on the straw helped keep them just warm enough to keep from even seeing their breath. "Colorado Territory definitely has its own charms."

"My sister says that the political people up in Denver have their eyes set on becoming a state before too long. They were hoping to do so before the end of the year, but it looks like it might be as late as spring now."

"You and your sister get along well."

A small sigh escaped him. "We did when we were younger. But after the war and my moving out here, we sort of lost touch with each other. Three years ago, when she and Mother followed me out this way, we sort of picked up right where we left off. It's been nice to know that time didn't age that relationship and make it into something less than it was."

"That's a blessing. If I had had a sibling, it would have been great to have a relationship like that."

He nodded, his eyes half-lidded as he pressed the back of his hand against his mouth in a yawn.

"You're tired," Charlotte said as she dropped the piece of straw she'd been holding and stood up from the bale. "We should get back inside. I'm sure you've had a long day."

He shrugged but stood, looking every bit as tired as she'd imagined. "I suppose you're right. It's just... sometimes it's nice to just sit and talk and forget about politics and the work that the town can bring on."

Her heart fluttered in her chest as she knocked some of the straw away from her skirts. She had hoped that she was supporting him and that he was enjoying their conversations as much as she had. But it had to have been more than an hour that they'd been sitting outside. The temperature had dropped a bit, but for some reason, their conversation and single oil lamp seemed to do enough to keep them warm. "Oh, I forgot to mention at dinner. I need to get more material from the haberdasher in the next day or two if possible. I've had three more orders for dresses for the ball. The two extras that I'd worked on both sold already."

He blinked at her. "That's amazing. Is everyone in the Temperance League ordering a dress for the ball then?"

"I'm not sure, but everyone in the bridge club is ordering one. Mrs. Francis certainly talked up my talents. I only hope that I can live up to the notoriety that she's creating for me."

"I'm sure you're just as good if not better than she's telling others. I've seen your dresses, and they are stunning to my untrained eye. But tomorrow isn't good, I'll take you into town the day after tomorrow if that's all right." He took hold of the lamp and then opened the barn door. A breeze blew in the chill and Charlotte pulled her wrap around her shoulders tighter. Then suddenly, he stepped closer to her, his handsome features coming into focus so very close to her. Her heart thrummed in her chest.

Then he leaned slightly to the side and picked a piece of straw off the side of her shawl. She allowed her breath to resume, trying not to be overloud in the exhale. But then his eyes met hers, and he was still so close, the fog of their breaths intermingled. His eyes were still hooded, a bit of tiredness around them, but in them burned something more, and her heart skipped a beat at the sight of it. Did he have affection for her, the way hers had been developing for him? Could she dare to hope that he could think of her as more than a just a friend and partner in this venture of mail-order marriage?

He leaned slightly toward her and for a moment, she had the fleeting thought that he might kiss her. Heat rushed to her cheeks as she closed her eyes and held her breath and waited. Then waited a little longer. Finally she allowed her eyes to open again, and found that he'd stepped back from her, his brow creased with worry. He cleared his throat. "Right, well. We should get back inside."

And disappointment filled her as he gestured for her to go ahead of him into the house. She did as he asked, but couldn't help the way that her heart sank toward her stomach. Maybe she hadn't seen what she thought she had in his eyes. Maybe she was wrong and was getting all excited over nothing by herself. Pulling her shawl closer, she headed inside.

TWO DAYS LATER, SIMON FOUND HIMSELF DRIVING THE cart with both his mother and Charlotte sitting on the bench seat next to him. Ever since he'd almost kissed her the night before last, he'd been avoiding Charlotte just a little. It was all too much for him to handle right now. Yes, he'd brought her in to be his wife. Yes, he'd been the one that decided that they should get to know each other by doing evening chores in the barn together—but... but what? How could he be so surprised that he'd started to develop feelings for her.

Charlotte was by far one of the most beautiful women that he'd ever laid eyes upon. And what was more was the fact that she was gentle and kind and completely unselfish. And she even got along smashingly well with his mother. He couldn't have asked for a better candidate to be his bride, but there was just something holding him back. What if she didn't feel the same way for him? What if he was boring her with these nightly talks—or if she was just doing what he said out of a sense of obligation. He'd hate that.

It pricked at his heart, just the thought of it.

Overhead, a blanket of clouds covered the sky, the air was crisp and clean, and definitely warned of snow. He didn't think that it would start too soon, but regardless, he'd try to push the two ladies along with their shopping so that he could return them home as soon as possible. If they only got a little bit, it wouldn't be too bad, but if it decided to snow in earnest, they might be in trouble with traveling back to the house. The clip-clop of Nugget's hooves against the gravel and stone roadway had a rhythm to them that helped Simon feel a little better. Since it was only the first week of December, it was a bit early for him to think about switching from the cart to the sleigh, but if they got measurable snow, that would make it a necessity.

By the time they reached town, the smallest of flurries began falling from the sky. Simon hopped down from the cart and then offered a hand to help each of the ladies down. Then he took the blanket they'd been using to cover their laps with and folded it and placed it back on the bench. "Do you think it will take you long to get the things you need from the haberdasher? I just need to head into the sheriff's office for just a moment to check on things but will leave the cart here at the hitching post while I do that instead of the livery if you won't be long."

"I think I shouldn't need more than a half hour, three-quarters of an hour at most," Charlotte said, white snowflakes sticking to her beautiful long lashes.

His heart thumped at how delicate her features were. But he swallowed those feelings back down and nodded and tied his reins to the hitching post. "That should be fine."

"Let's shop quickly, then," his mother said as she guided Charlotte toward the haberdashery.

Simon watched the two of them for a moment before turning and heading towards the sheriff's office. Movement to his left caught his eye, and he watched as a big man in dark clothing with two others stepped into the livery that Simon had not wanted to go toward. He frowned. What was Jeb Holt and his ilk doing in town?

Was there a Cattleman's Association meeting that Simon didn't know about? Not likely. Mr. Francis had been informing him of meetings lately to be sure that Simon was in attendance and able to at least make a presence for the sake of the voters there. Curious, Simon headed toward the livery as the flurries of snow and suspicion continued to swirl around him. When he got to the doorway, he hesitated. Something inside him told him that he shouldn't enter through the normal route. So instead, he turned to the side of the barn, climbed over the paddock fence there and then snuck into one of the side doors of the stalls that were open into the paddock. Keeping low with his body, he was able to sneak in, hoping that the squelching of his boots in the inch-deep mud wouldn't make anyone aware of his presence. He ducked into the stall and drew next to the stall door, closer to the sound of hushed voices.

"It's not good enough," Jeb Holt said. "There are still too many supporters for Harris and the election is just a fortnight away. I need to put the last nail into the coffin, and this will do it."

"The snow will make a good cover," one of the lackeys said. "Not too many people out and about."

"Exactly," the other one said. "Dirk and Scotty are locking up the sheriff's office as we speak and then we'll be ready."

"Good. We need to make this bank job fast and get out of town as quickly as possible," Holt said with a sneer in his voice. "Let's make this Harris look like the fool he is. When the bank in Franktown gets robbed right under his nose and he can't do anything about it, it will only make me look that much better."

"Yeah, it was genius you let me and Colton get caught by you only to get rescued by the rest of our crew on the way to the sheriff."

Simon swallowed. So, this had all been part of a plot all along, and Tom Crowley, the bounty hunter, had been right when he'd said the ringleader was local. It seems that it was Jeb Holt the whole time. What would he do in their county once he had control of it as sheriff? Simon shuddered at the thought. He started to back away, keeping his head low still when the front door to the livery shoved open a bit and two more voices joined the group.

"It's done," one with a deep voice said. "The sheriff's office doors are locked up tight. But I'm not sure the sheriff was there."

One of the other henchmen laughed. "Don't matter none. If he has the gall to show up alone, it just gives us reason to put a bullet into him. Then boss'll win the election by default."

"Y'all better keep an eye out for him," the deep voiced one said. "We don't have much time once we begin."

"Then you men better get started," Jeb Holt said. "And I'll keep watch from here."

Where was Sam, the livery man for all this? Simon's heart pounded in his chest as he snuck out the side door of the barn, looking in all directions to make sure that he wasn't spotted. What was he going to do now? He needed to make it to the sheriff's office without being seen and get his deputies to the bank. But how was he going to do that when he had to pass the livery doors to make it to the the sheriff's office? He was outnumbered five to one right now and he couldn't possibly walk past without being spotted and consequently captured. Or killed. Chances were, these men were responsible for Mr. Frank Smith's death, at least.

As he came over the livery fence again, Nugget

spotted him and nickered. He wasn't far from where he'd tied the gelding to the hitching post outside the haberdashery. The haberdasher. A plan formed in his mind. He hated to put anyone else in danger, but he knew this was likely the best way to make everyone safe. So, he started toward the store.

CHAPTER 10

Charlotte had just set a bolt of blue fabric on the counter when the bell above the door jingled and the sheriff entered the haberdashery, his gaze fixed on her. Her heart skipped a beat at the intensity of his glare.

"Simon?" Mabel asked from behind her. "Is something wrong?"

The wrinkles in his brow were deeper than Charlotte had ever seen them. "We have an emergency," he said, his gaze darting toward the door again before coming back to them. "The bank is about to get robbed. I just heard the full plot from all the men involved as they'd met in the livery."

Mr. Drake, the haberdasher, frowned and then

reached down below the counter and pulled out a shotgun. "What do you need help with, sheriff?"

The sheriff shook his head. "We'd need more than just you and me. I count at least five men involved in the robbery. Besides, I can't have a bunch of armed civilians risking their lives in a possible shootout. I mean—how good of a shot are you to start with?"

One of Mr. Drake's brows lifted. "I served under General Joseph Hooker at the battle of Fredericksburg."

The wrinkles over Simon's brow softened a bit as his eyes widened. "I didn't know that, sir. Forgive my ignorance."

"We don't talk much about the war here in Franktown, now, but several of the men in town served. I know at least three that are at hand and ready to come under your command if you so will it, sheriff."

"Three? Are they nearby... on this side of the livery?"

"I have but to get word to the barber's shop next door and we'll have three, possibly more armed and ready."

The sheriff looked impressed. "Is there any chance that one of you have a sniper's rifle?"

Mr. Drake huffed a laugh. "I have one myself, upstairs. I can't see as well as I used to in order to shoot it with iron sights, though."

"I can shoot it."

This time it was Mr. Drake's turn to look impressed. "You have training in sharpshooting, sir?"

Simon nodded.

"Then I'll be back directly with that rifle." He dashed away.

Charlotte finally spoke up, her voice shaking but filled with her determination. "I'll go the barbershop."

The wrinkles in Simon's brow returned. "I can't ask you to do that."

She shook her head. "You're not asking me to. I'm volunteering. It's not safe for you to go out there. If one of the robbers sees the sheriff moving around town, they'll know something is wrong and it will make them harm you or change their plans. And how often does the haberdasher leave his store in the middle of the day in order to go to the barbershop? I can't help but feel that if I go, I'll draw less suspicion. They aren't likely to pay much attention to a woman walking from one shop to another."

"It's too dangerous. There's no way that I can allow you to go alone out there," Simon said.

"She won't be alone," Mabel said. "I'll go with her."

"Absolutely not. I can't have the two of you going off and heading into danger like that. If there's a shootout or something goes wrong... if the two of you look even the least bit suspicious. What if... What if things go horribly wrong?" Simon had begun to sound panicked.

Mabel stepped up and put a hand on his arm. "It'll be all right, son. Charlotte is right. If you or Mr. Drake go, you're much more likely to draw attention. If the two of us go together and laugh and act naturally, the men are going to ignore us. This is the best and safest plan for everyone."

He took hold of the hand on his arm and put it between both of his. "If something happens to you..." His worried gaze slipped over to Charlotte too, "to either of you, I will never forgive myself."

This time it was Charlotte's turn to step forward and put a hand on his arm. "We'll be all right. I promise that I will take care of you mother."

He shook his head at her, his eyes pleading and his voice cracking as he whispered, "I don't want anything to happen to either of you."

"Be reasonable," Mabel said, raising her chin. "If you let your emotions cloud your judgement, then we should all stay here and let them rob the bank and leave town without incident. The bad guys will succeed, and you will be branded a coward for hiding with womenfolk in the haberdashery."

Charlotte blinked at Mabel for saying such a thing, but Simon laughed and shook his head. "You're right mother. We can't have everyone thinking that I hide behind my mother's apron now, can we?"

Mabel patted his shoulder with a smile and then held out her elbow. "Now, Charlotte, please take hold of my arm and let us support each other as we go out. We're just taking a jaunty stroll over to the barber's. Nothing to see here. Do be sure to laugh at my joking."

Nodding, Charlotte stepped over and hooked her elbow in Mabel's. "Whether you say something funny or not, I will be sure to chuckle." Then she met eyes with Simon. "Nothing to worry about. We will take care of each other."

Even though he smiled softly as he watched them, the worry in his eyes hadn't subsided at all. But still, she and Mabel turned around and pushed the door to the shop open and stepped out into the breezy swirls of snowflakes. Somehow it felt a bit colder outside than it had earlier. Immediately,

Charlotte was struck with the temptation to look around, but she knew that would seem suspicious, so she kept her eyes focused on Mabel and upon the way in front of them. They only needed to walk a few yards from the haberdashery to the barber's. Certainly, they could do that without drawing too much suspicion.

"Keep our eyes down and smiles in place. And laugh," Mabel said more to herself than to Charlotte and followed it up with a hearty chuckle and loudly followed it with, "Can you believe it?"

Playing along, Charlotte widened her eyes and shook her head. "No!" she said incredulously. "I never would have thought."

Then the two of them chuckled together, holding each other's arms tightly as they continued forward. Charlotte saw a dark movement across the street from the corner of her eye but didn't want to turn her head that direction. There weren't many people on the street due to the weather, and chances were that it was one of the five men the sheriff had warned them about. It was best to assume that it was and not meet eyes with anyone.

After taking three or four more steps, they were in front of the barber's and they immediately slipped inside the doorway. The bell overhead jingled and the three men who'd been sitting in chairs immediately stood with mouths agape and eyes wide. The barber just stared for a long moment, scissors in one hand and comb in the other. Then he regained his faculties. "Could I... um... help you two ladies?"

Mabel stepped forward. "I'm the sheriff's mother, and this is his fiancé. We were just in the haberdashery. The sheriff has learned of a plot where there are at least five men involved to rob the bank. The way to the sheriff's office is blocked."

The men continued to stand with their mouths agape.

Charlotte joined Mabel. "Mr. Drake has gotten his rifle and shotgun and has asked which of you will help him in joining the sheriff to stop these villains?"

Finally, that drew the men's attentions and they fisted their hands and nodded. "Hear, hear."

The barber said, "I have two rifles as well. Bob, do you have a pistol?"

"I do." One of the other men, presumably Bob, nodded and pulled back his jacket to expose the weapon on his side.

Once the barber had set aside his scissors and comb, he rushed over toward the countertop and pulled out his two rifles, handing one to each of the other two men. "I believe I have my service revolver upstairs."

He ran up the stairs and returned soon after with the pistol. Then the four of them started for the door. Charlotte and Mabel went to follow, but Bob held up a hand. "It's not safe out there for you. Please stay here."

"Yes," the barber said, his brow wrinkled. "You two ladies have done enough just to get us. We'll join the sheriff at the haberdashery. You two stay here and remain safe."

At some point in time, Mabel and Charlotte had linked arms again, as though their bodies knew that they needed comfort and attracted to one another like wet sheets on a laundry line. Charlotte met eyes with the older woman who nodded. Then Charlotte returned her gaze to the men. "All right. We'll wait here as long as you let the sheriff know that we both arrived in good health."

"We will let him know," Bob said, and then the group of them ducked out the doorway.

Charlotte squeezed Mabel's arm and swallowed hard, her mind already imagining the danger that these men were all putting themselves through in order to save the town. And Simon was at the center of it. "Oh Lord, please keep them all safe."

Then Mabel hugged Charlotte's arm. "Let's do what we can to help and pray."

Nodding, Charlotte joined Mabel as they both went down to their knees.

SIMON HAD TAKEN MR. DRAKE'S SNIPER RIFLE AND went to the second floor of the building and sat in the window. He remained behind the curtain until he was certain that no one was looking in his direction. Then he used the iron sights to focus on the lock and chain that someone had placed on the door of the sheriff's office. If he could shoot the lock, he could at least free the men inside. Luckily it was not one of the railroad grade locks that would have taken at least two or three shots from his rifle in order to disengage. If it had been an Alfred Hobbs lock, he'd have had to abandon the idea all together. But as it was, the cattle-chain lock was easy to disengage in one hit, provided that he actually made the target.

It had been a while since Simon had need of his sharpshooting skills. He'd played at practicing for years in his yard on his own acreage, but was he still capable of a shot like this? He softly sent up a prayer as he focused in on his target. And trusting that the rifle wouldn't be off in any direction, he slowly exhaled and prepared to pull the trigger when shots were fired downstairs.

Glass shattered, and Simon's heart leapt into his throat. What was going on down there? Had the men from the barbershop come? Sweat beaded on his forehead, and black dots crowded his vision, but he dared not look away from the target he had in his sights. He had one chance and he needed to take it. No matter how many men they had downstairs willing to help in this bank robbery fiasco, he needed the deputies in his office as well. Pushing aside the fear and dots and everything else, he prayed as he exhaled and pulled the trigger.

The bullet hit the cattle-chain lock dead on, nearly snapping it in half as it disengaged and fell from one side of the chain. Immediately, one of the deputies burst through the door and onto the street, one side of the chain sliding through the door handle and falling to the side, out of the way. Then the deputy pulled his pistol and started firing in the direction of the bank.

That was enough. Simon hopped up from his knees and rushed down the stairs to the first floor. Drake and four others were standing at the busted-out windows and firing their weapons. Simon shouted, "Hold your fire!"

The men stopped and there were a couple more pops of gunfire out in the street before they stopped too.

"We need to see what's going on," Simon said. "We can't just fire willy-nilly or some bystander might get hurt."

"Yes, sheriff," one of the newcomers from the barbershop said.

Nodding, Simon stepped over the broken glass on the floor of the shop and started for the door. He opened it and peered out. The street was barren and silent. Stepping out farther, he met eyes with the three deputies who'd made their way out of the office. He waved his hat toward them, and they started toward his direction. Once they saw him shake his head once, the three of them froze in their tracks. "Could you men please come with me," Simon called behind him.

"Yes, sir," Mr. Drake said, and all five of them scrambled up behind him.

He gestured for the group to stay close to the wall as they made their way toward the livery. When he glanced at the deputies, they were also hugging the walls and making their way closer. Knowing that

Jeb Holt might still be hiding inside, Simon kicked open the door and waved his pistol in, but only found an empty stable. Once he was certain that they were not in danger there, he led the men toward the bank. The six of them stood on one side of the door and the three deputies on the other. He called over to Deputy Marcus, "Did you see the robbers? Are they still inside?"

Marcus nodded. "Yes sir."

"How many?"

"I counted four, sir."

Four. Not five. Did that mean that there was still someone out here, or had someone already made it inside before the deputy started counting? Just then, in answer to his unspoken question, a bullet grazed past his face and hit the wall, splintering the wood in all directions. "Get down!"

And in answer, all of the men got down on the ground as they were peppered with four more bullets. Gritting his teeth, Simon determined where the gunfire was coming from. "The hay loft at the livery."

Nodding, Marcus leapt to his feet, and one of the other deputies followed suit. They dashed toward the livery doors. When one of the other men tried to get up to join them, Simon shook his head.

"Wait," he told them. One more gunshot came from the loft of the barn and then Simon knew that the pistol was empty. He leapt to his feet. "Let the deputies get the lone gunman in the loft. We'll need all of you together to stop this robbery."

The men nodded and then Simon made a move to kick in the door of the bank.

BLOOD OOZED THROUGH MABEL'S FINGERS, AND Charlotte thought she might faint for a moment from the panic. "You've been hit!" she cried.

But Mabel shook her head. "It was the glass, not a bullet."

"Oh, thank the Lord," Charlotte said, as she feared the worst, but still, knew that the wound was serious from the amount of blood. "Hold pressure on it, and I'll get some iodine."

It was fortuitous that they were still in the barbershop. Since barbers often acted as dentists and did minor doctoring, she knew that there was likely to be a tincture of iodine somewhere, and she found the small red bottle not far from where the barber had set down his scissors. After taking hold of it, Charlotte found a clean cloth and then returned to her knees at Mabel's side.

The sleeve just above Mabel's wrist had been cut and the glass had made a clean slice right through several layers of the skin on her arm. Charlotte wiped the area clean and then poured the tincture on it. "This will sting badly for a moment, but then it will dull the nerves."

Mabel hissed and nodded. "Do you have your sewing kit with you?"

Every seamstress worth their salt also learned the proper technique for making sutures. Charlotte took hold of the small pouch she'd had attached to the sleeve of her jacket and pulled out the needle and thread she had in the kit there. Then she went to work, putting in seven stitches across the clean cut. The plate glass window of the barbershop had shattered soon after the men had left the building. Unfortunately, the men had looked a bit more suspicious than Charlotte and Mabel had when they were out on the street.

Once the sutures were done, she found some gauze where the iodine had been, and wrapped it well to keep the pressure on. Frowning she met eyes with Mabel. "We promised that we wouldn't get hurt."

"Pish-posh," Mabel said with a wave of her hand. "This is nothing. I could have done this with a knife in the kitchen while peeling potatoes. It's not bad and it will heal quickly. But things aren't over yet."

The gunfire had stopped for a moment, but while Charlotte was suturing, a few more shots were made. She frowned as she looked outside. "What should we do?"

"Continue with what we were doing. We need to get back to praying."

Charlotte met eyes with the older woman, who nodded to her. Bowing her head, Charlotte knew that Mabel was right. There was nothing greater that they could do for the men outside than to cover them with prayers. They determined that until the gunfire was long over, they would stay there on their knees.

SIMON LET OUT A SIGH OF RELIEF ONCE ALL OF THE robbers were captured and they'd taken control of the bank again. The man who'd been shooting from the hayloft was none other than Jeb Holt. Now that all five of the gang were in custody, Simon could breathe easy. He left the men in the charge of his deputies, and after shaking hands with each of the citizens who'd helped them, he marched directly toward the barbershop. His stomach sank as soon as he saw the broken glass of the windows there as he approached. If something had happened to either of them he'd never forgive himself. His mother didn't need to be endangered, but when he thought of Charlotte, his heart squeezed even further in his chest.

Honest and brave, Charlotte didn't deserve to be hurt in something like this. Maybe he didn't deserve to feel the way he did about her, but he was afraid that he'd already grown too attached to just let her go. He looked forward to spending time with her. Her smile was enough to make all of the stress in his life go away. If she was hurt, he didn't know what he'd do.

Cracking glass reached his ears as the two ladies stepped out of the barbershop and into the street. They were alive. But his relief was short lived, when he saw that they were both covered in blood. His heart jumped into his throat, and he had to swallow back that feeling as he asked. "Who is hurt? Were you shot?"

They both looked up at him, his mother smiling, but Charlotte's brow remained wrinkled. "We're both fine, son," his mother said. "I just got a little cut on the glass is all."

"The glass?" he asked, looking toward Charlotte. "But you have blood all over your arms, too."

"I stitched up your mother's wound, she has a two-inch incision on her arm just above her wrist caused by the plate glass of the window. I'm sorry."

He frowned. "Why are you sorry?"

Unshed tears shined in Charlotte's eyes. "I didn't keep your mother safe. She was hurt anyway. I tried, but—"

A smile came unbidden to his lips, and he couldn't help but step forward and pull her into his embrace. Her body stiffened at first, but then she relaxed and melted into his arms, as her own arms wrapped around him. Immediately, she sobbed into his chest.

He stroked her back and hair and said to her, "It's all right. Everything is fine now. You're safe, my mother's safe, and that's all that matters. I'm sorry that you had to go through all of this."

She shook her head against his chest but didn't pull away. Then she mumbled something.

"What was that? I didn't understand you."

After turning her head, she said again. "Thank

you for saying that. I love that you knew just what to say to make me feel better."

At the sound of that word... love... something inside Simon just fell right into place. He pulled back from her just enough to look into her eyes. He searched the unfathomable gray depths of them and then said, "Charlotte, I love you."

She blinked at him, flinching just a little as if what he'd said hurt her. For a long moment, he held his breath, waiting for what she might tell him. His fragile heart prepared itself to be shattered. Then she smiled slightly and said, "I love you too, Simon."

Heat rose up the back of his neck, but his fragile heart needed to know. "Are you sure?"

A laugh bubbled up and her brows wrinkled for a moment. Then she shook her head. "Of course I'm certain. I love you Simon Harris. I love how you take care of your mother and this town, and even your horse, but forget yourself. I love how you chew on a piece of straw sometimes when you're talking, and how you fight your tiredness just to be with me and get to know me. There's so much about you to love, that I don't understand how you can doubt it."

His own chest shook as he huffed a laugh of his own. "Then, you'll stay here in Franktown and be my wife?"

"I will."

And when she said it, a floodgate of emotion struck Simon so that he couldn't help but place a hand upon her cheek and lean forward, brushing his lips across hers. Then they met eyes for a moment, and he could see the passion that he felt reflected there in her eyes. He leaned in and kissed her again, longer and deeper this time, the whole world spinning around them and growing farther away.

Until his mother cleared her throat.

And they both pulled back from each other.

"I was wondering when you two would realize that I was still standing here." She smiled up at them both. "And besides, you both should save some of that for after the wedding."

More heat rose to Simon's cheeks as he stole a glance at his future bride. Happiness filled his soul and his heart suddenly felt less fragile. Instead of being made of glass, it seemed to be hardening and softening at the same time. He'd been afraid to trust anyone with his heart, but now he felt for sure that he could rely upon Charlotte to keep his heart safe. And in return he would give her every bit of love he could, because she deserved it.

EPILOGUE

Satisfaction filled Charlotte as she took Simon's hand and allowed him to help her into the sleigh attached to Nugget. Two days before Christmas Eve, they'd gotten over eight inches of snow which allowed them to attach the very different cart apparatus to the palomino. Before the night of the ball, Charlotte had never ridden in one of these.

"Aren't you coming?" Simon asked his mother.

Mabel shook her head and adjusted her festive hat. "Come back and get me after you all take a trip around town once on your own. I want to speak to Mrs. Francis for just a moment."

He lifted a brow. "Are you sure?"

She laughed and whispered something in his ear.

A wide smile spread across his lips and then he nodded and hopped into the sleigh. Once they were sitting next to each other, Simon gave her a little peck on the cheek. "Are you warm enough?"

Snuggled under the fur blanket, Charlotte nodded. "I am."

"Good," he said and clucked at Nugget to get him to move forward.

The wind picked up as they went along and down the street, the sleigh sliding across the snow with a swishing noise. That Christmas Eve had been the most satisfying night of Charlotte's life as eight of the dresses that she designed and made were worn in the ball. She'd never seen so many pretty things, and she'd done her best to make each dress unique to the wearer.

Her face stung a bit as the breeze made her eyes water and the water stayed upon her cheeks, chilling her. She shivered.

Leaning toward her, Simon asked, "Are you sure you're all right?"

Charlotte looped her arms around his and snuggled closer to him, feeling the warmth of his body. "I am better than all right."

After Jeb Holt's trial, Simon won the election for town sheriff uncontested. And soon after they'd had their wedding. They had been married for two full weeks now, and it had been a joyous time for Charlotte. For the first time in her life, she felt complete and truly satisfied. It was amazing to her that a little more than two months ago, she thought her life had fallen apart, but instead, everything had fallen into place. God had guided her toward something better.

"Whoa," Simon called out and pulled the reins, stopping Nugget.

Charlotte blinked. They weren't back at the Francis house, but on Main Street. "What's going on?"

Instead of answering, he nodded toward the building where they were parked, between the barbershop and the stagecoach office. There, in the small space with a wide window, a wooden mannequin stood. Charlotte gasped and stood from her seat. "Where did they get that thing? They are so expensive. Mr. Montgomery had one in his shop, but even in Washington they are considered rare."

"Mrs. Francis said that we should get one for your shop, so I had it delivered from Denver."

She froze and then turned toward him. "Did you just say, 'my shop?'"

He nodded. "I didn't know what you wanted to call it, so I didn't get a sign made yet."

She sat back down, staring into space, not sure what to think. "My shop... and my own mannequin." She turned and met eyes with Simon. "Really? All mine?"

He nodded. "You deserve it."

Her vision went blurry as she wrapped her arms around him in a hug and held tight for a long moment. "I can't believe it. Thank you so much."

"Merry Christmas," he said as he hugged her back.

Then she pulled away with a frown. "But I didn't get you anything."

He laughed and shook his head. "You married me, and that is better than any present you could have given me."

She couldn't help but hug him again. "I love you so much, Simon."

"And I'm so happy that you do."

Pulling back, she quirked an eyebrow at him.

"Oh, and I love you too, Charlotte."

Smiling, she said, "That's better."

Then she snuggled up next to him and looked at the mannequin in the window, still marveling at it.

"Are you ready to go?" he asked.

"Just five more minutes. I just want to stare at it a bit longer."

"All right," he said as he pulled the blanket up over her again to make sure she stayed warm. And then he waited for ten minutes before they finally pulled away.

THE END

AFTERWORD

AND ABOUT THE SERIES

Thank you for reading Simon's story!

This is the second in a series of Christmas Mail-Order Bride stories that I will be releasing over the next year or so. There are seven in total, with three releasing this season, so be on the look out for them!

At the same time, I'm releasing a boxed set of some of my older Christmas mail-order bride stories that were originally part of other multi-author series. My editors and I are working on giving them one more workup and then adding an epilogue to a few as well.

I hope you'll check out the rest of this series of

Western Historical Holiday Romances, as each one will have a bride arriving by stagecoach, and will be a clean, wholesome, standalone novella written from a Christian worldview. Every story will have a happily ever after and feature down-to-earth characters with real world problems who overcome them by grace and love.

Can unexpected Christmas magic spark love's flame between a man with no bride and the woman who has traveled so far to win his wary affection?

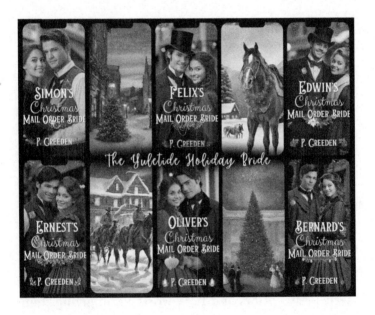

ABOUT THE AUTHOR

P. Creeden is the sweet romance and mystery pen name for USA Today Bestselling Author, Pauline Creeden. Her stories feature down-to-earth characters who often feel like they are undeserving of love for one reason or another and are surprised when love finds them.

Animals are the supporting characters of many of her stories, because they occupy her daily life on the farm, too. From dogs, cats, and goldfish to horses, chickens, and geckos -- she believes life around pets is so much better, even if they are fictional. P. Creeden married her college sweetheart, who she also met at a horse farm. Together they raise a menagerie of animals and their one son, an avid reader, himself.

If you enjoyed this story, look forward to more books by P. Creeden.
In 2024, she plans to release more than 12 new books!
Hear about her newest release, FREE books when they come available, and giveaways hosted by the author—subscribe to her newsletter:
https://www.subscribepage.com/pcreedenbooks

Join the My Beta and ARC reader Group on Facebook!
I publish a new story every other month on average!

If you enjoyed this book and want to help the author, consider leaving a review at your favorite book seller – or tell someone about it on social media. Authors live by word of mouth!

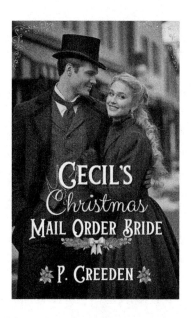

This Christmas, love arrives unexpectedly in Idaho Springs —by stagecoach.

December 1887 - When mail-order bride and nurse Gwendolyn Wright steps off the stagecoach, she expects a new beginning as bride to Idaho Springs' handsome young doctor, Cecil Cody. But Dr. Cody seems oblivious to their matrimonial arrangement. As snow blankets the dusty streets this Christmas, Gwendolyn discovers more trouble than tidings in this untamed town. Suspicion and rumors plague her efforts to bring holiday spirit and health to the sick townspeople.

The unlikely pair must learn to heal wounds and soften hearts for misunderstandings to unravel. Can unexpected Christmas magic spark love's flame between a man with no bride and the woman who has traveled so far to win his wary affection?

This is a clean, wholesome, standalone novella written from a Christian worldview. It has a happily ever after and features down-to-earth characters with real world problems who overcome them by grace and love.

Get your copy of Cecil's Christmas Mail-Order Bride!

And check out the rest of the books in the Historical Western Holiday Romance Series!

FIRST CHAPTER OF CECIL'S
CHRISTMAS MAIL-ORDER BRIDE

Cecil Cody opened the door of his clinic to allow his mother to walk through before grabbing her steamer trunk from behind her and rolling it out the door before pulling it shut.

"I wish you could stay longer, Mother. Two weeks was not nearly long enough," he said as he helped her down the steps of the wide wooden porch before going back to get the trunk again.

His mother lifted a brow. "Do you really? You're much too busy, and I felt that I was getting in your way more than anything. After all, I don't know enough about nursing to be of any real help to you."

"I haven't had time to send out an advertisement to bring a nurse in. I need to do that." The wind picked up again, bringing with it a bit more chill than Cecil had prepared for. He rubbed his arms for warmth.

Pulling the collar of her jacket up closer to her chin, his mother gestured toward his front door. "You're in such a hurry to get rid of me that you've forgotten your coat."

Feeling admonished, he bowed his head and stomped toward the door. His mother had a way of making him feel like a child again. He quickly opened the door and grabbed his hat and coat from the hooks just inside, and then shoved his hat on his head before swinging his coat over his shoulders and pushing his arms through. "Honestly, Mother, I wish you would stay longer. Even though I've been busy with work, I've enjoyed our meals together, and there's always a chance that my time would open up."

"Doubtful," she said, pulling her gloves on. "Besides, I want to visit with your sister, Marie, and her family in Denver for a while before heading back to Oregon. I'd love to stay with her till Christmas, but I don't think your father would like that very much."

"I wish you could have talked him into coming too."

"So do I," she said with a sigh, "But he and your

uncle have been busy with the harvest of grapes from the vineyards and will be barreling wine for the next few weeks. It's just not the right time of year."

Cecil mumbled under his breath, "It never seems to be the right time of year."

His mother laid a hand on his shoulder. "Your father tends to throw himself into his work, much like you do, since you take after him. It's as difficult for him to leave Oregon as it is for you to leave Colorado. We both would have wished that you could have opened a practice closer..."

"Yes, Mother, but this is where I got the call. The miners here needed a doctor."

She nodded and waved a hand in front of her. "I know. I'm just expressing a wish, not trying to nag you. At least you're nearby your sister now. Anyway, get my trunk, or I'll be late for my stagecoach. You will come down for a day or two for Thanksgiving? Your sister expects you to come."

Cecil shrugged but nodded at the same time. "I'll try my best."

"You had better. It's not as if you have a wife here to cook you a good meal for Thanksgiving, or every evening for that matter. You need someone to look after you like I've been doing the past couple weeks. You need to get married."

This conversation again? Cecil's hand fisted around the trunk's handle as he reminded himself that he truly was going to miss his mother though at times she could be frustrating. "I'll be fine mother. I just need a nurse to help me with the work, and I'll have more time to eat proper meals at home instead of trying to catch them at the cafe."

His mother pursed her lips and shook her head. "That cafe uses too much salt in all their meals. I swear they are just trying to get you to pay more for drinks."

"It's fine, Mother. But if it will make you happy, I'll ask them to go easy on my meals when it comes to the salt."

She nodded her approval, and then the two of them walked down the street to the Idaho Springs stagecoach office where they were already loading for the trip to Denver. Cecil helped the coachman with his mother's trunk and then, since he was there, he helped load the rest of the luggage for other passengers as well. Once finished, he turned to his mother, wiping the sweat from his brow. "I'll do my best to come down for Thanksgiving. I have more motivation, since I know you'll still be there."

"You had better," his mother said, resting a hand on his shoulder and leaning in to receive a kiss on the cheek.

Cecil obliged and kissed his mother's soft cheek. She smelled of lavender and powder, scents that he remembered from his childhood. He had thought all women smelled this way, or at least should, back then. Then she gave him a quick embrace before taking the coachman's hand as he helped her into the stage.

He withdrew his hat, hoping to cool off as the stage started to pull away. The wind pulled the sweat from his brow, but he could tell he still had more under his coat from the exertion of helping with the luggage. The sun still sat low on the horizon, and the rest of the town would just be getting up to start their day. He didn't know why his mother insisted on taking the earliest possible stagecoach out of town, but he imagined if she'd gone later in the day, he would have had a harder time seeing her off. Perhaps it was for the best that she left early. He waved toward the coach as it pulled farther away. He didn't see anyone wave back, and wasn't even certain his mother was looking, but it made him feel better that if she did look, he was waving toward her.

When the stagecoach was fully out of sight, he

let out a long breath. Then he unbuttoned his jacket to let the air in and started walking back toward his clinic. His mind was already reeling with all the things he needed to get done before seeing his first patient that day. He had a couple of appointments before noon, then he'd be heading out to the miner's camp afterward to see to the injured men he'd been dressing wounds for. A long day stared him in the face, but somehow, the busyness excited him and kept him on his toes. He was ready to take on the day with full fervor. But first, coffee.

GWENDOLYN WRIGHT'S FINGERS WERE WRINKLED, AND her hands felt scalded from the hot water that she worked with as she scrubbed laundry. She sighed and wiped the sweat from her brow. They didn't tell her in the Richmond Nursing School that once she finished the program, there'd be no jobs for nurses nearby. So instead, she found herself working in the hospital's laundry room. Sadly, she didn't even need her degree in nursing in order to work there.

A bell rang overhead, and even though it was distant, people immediately responded to it. Everyone dropped what they were doing and headed for the door. The shift was over. She followed them, wiping her hands on her apron, and flexing her fingers, trying to get the achiness out of them, and continued to do so as she stood in line. When she reached the desk of the supervisor, she signed out on her time card and then continued up the stairs and out of the hospital basement. After nodding goodbye to some of the other ladies who worked laundry with her, she started walking through the fading sunlight toward her home in downtown Richmond. The streets at dusk were full of people heading home from a hard day's work, as well as children running and playing after school and before dinner. Her stomach growled at the thought of dinner, but she just rubbed her midsection and continued walking. The few trees in yards here and there had empty branches, and she crunched over the dried leaves as she stepped past them on the sidewalk. When she reached her building, she sighed.

For the past year, she'd been sharing a one room apartment with another girl who was without family and earning a nursing degree as well. But the life that her roommate had been living was far different from the one she had. Having no family around anymore to help her had made Gwendolyn completely self-sufficient. Even though her family had left her enough money for a boarding house while she was in school and for her education, that money had completely dried up a year ago, and she'd had to look for other arrangements. Madeline had offered that they get an apartment together when they'd graduated. Now, Gwendolyn worked all day, scrubbing sheets and linens for the hospital, and barely made enough to pay rent and get by.

Her roommate, on the other hand, slept all day and then painted her face in makeup and went out all night. In some ways, it helped that they could hot-bunk. They could both sleep in the bed all to themselves because their schedules were so different. Though Gwendolyn didn't know exactly what Madeline, her roommate, was doing through the night, she had a few guesses, and none of them were good.

She caught sight of Madeline coming down the steps as she was heading up. Madeline's hair was coiffed perfectly in place, and her made-up face made her look gaudy and different. Not necessarily prettier, but somehow appealing. When Madeline saw her, she smiled and hopped down the last few steps. "I got paid extra for a job last night, so I bought some ham. There's some in the fridge if you want to use it in a soup for yourself. I just ate it as it was, but I know you'd probably rather cook it."

Gwendolyn's stomach grumbled happily at the thought of getting to eat something other than bread and vegetables. Her mouth even began to water. "Thank you," was all that she could say. Though she didn't approve of how her roommate was living outside of their apartment together, she couldn't help but wonder if Madeline was at least living a better life.

Madeline had more money, seemed to be sleeping more, and spending more time having fun. At least her joints didn't seem to ache, and her fingers didn't get wrinkles from being soaked in hot water all day. And then there was the fact that at least Madeline got to eat meat once in a while. Maybe it would be better for Gwendolyn to give in to Madeline's offer to start in her business. But no. She shook her head as she remembered the Psalm about envying the prosperity of the wicked. It wasn't that she felt that Madeline was wicked, Gwendolyn knew that she was not. But Gwendolyn also knew that Madeline was playing with fire as she went out at night. And that wasn't something that Gwendolyn needed to get involved in.

As she finished passing by her friend, she asked

God for forgiveness for her momentary jealousy, for her temptation to choose comfort over righteous living, and for the safety of her friend as she went out that night. Thinking of Madeline, Gwendolyn turned around and looked for her again, but Madeline was already long gone. She bowed her head and prayed for her friend again. Prayed that Madeline would turn away from her nightly activities and live a better life, and that she would be kept safe from the whims of those who might mistreat her as she continued down the path she was taking.

Gwendolyn didn't want to judge her friend, knowing that it wasn't her job to judge, but she did want to love her friend, and so she did what she could to help her friend survive while she prayed and hoped to live by example. But was all of that really enough? Was it the best course of action?

Didn't Madeline's mother admonish and punish her enough for the life she'd chosen? They were completely estranged now, neither of them speaking to the other, and acting as though the other was dead. If Gwendolyn had taken the mother's side, it wouldn't have helped, but just strained and perhaps broken the relationship they had together as it was. Instead, Gwendolyn had chosen to pray and love. She could only hope she was doing the right thing.

After she made it to their fourth-floor apartment, Gwendolyn took the hambone which still had a bit of ham left on it and stuck it into a pot with lentils. The one room apartment was a little chilly since the building hadn't put on the heat yet—it wasn't quite cold enough. Instead, the radiator sat cold in the alcove by the window, waiting to be turned on. So, she warmed her hands at the stove top while the soup warmed and couldn't wait to start eating. After fetching her bible, she set it on the table next to the newspaper so that she could study while waiting on things to cook. But soon after she sat down, there was a loud knocking at the door that made Gwen's heart jump in her chest.

Blinking, she stepped toward the door. "Who is it?"

"Madeline! I know you're in there, you harlot! Get out here with my money right now," a gruff voice said on the other side.

Fearful, Gwendolyn kept a distance from the door. "Madeline isn't here. I'm alone and will not be opening the door."

"Liar!" The man called out and banged against the door again. "I know she's in there. She was supposed to meet me at the club tonight with my money. I waited half an hour for her, and I will not be played the fool. Open this door now or I will make you both sorry for it."

The banging started up again, rattling the heavy wooden door on its very hinges. Gwendolyn clutched her chest. "I promise you, sir. Madeline is not here."

"What good is a harlot's promise? If I can't get my money out of her, I'll get it out of you just the same."

Now Gwen's fear truly took hold. She wasn't a harlot. She wasn't even certain that Madeline was. But was she? Gwendolyn couldn't firmly say no to that question either. But regardless, this man had put her in the same occupation as Madeline simply because they lived together. A lump formed in Gwendolyn's throat and tears stung the backs of her eyes. She swallowed it all back as she tried again. "I assure you, sir. I have no money."

The banging grew louder, and a couple of thumps hit the door as she could only imagine the man attempted to batter against it with his shoulder. Not knowing what else to do, Gwendolyn took her bible from off the table and hugged it to her chest. Then she began to pray. She prayed for the strength of the door to hold against the man's railings. She prayed that somehow, God would take this man away from her door. But as she prayed, she also came to the realization that she couldn't live here anymore. This was the last night that she should live in this hovel like this. Obviously, God wasn't pleased with her living arrangement, and this was his way of telling her just that.

Things grew quiet outside her door for a moment, and there was a murmuring of conversation in the hallway. Had Mr. Miller from across the hallway put a stop to the man's railings? Curious, Gwendolyn stepped closer to the door and leaned an ear against it, trying to find out what was being said.

"Don't think this is over," the man growled right on the other side of the wood. "I'll return for what's mine."

Then he banged his fist against the door one last time, making Gwendolyn jump and back away a step. Footsteps receded and then there was a gentler knock against the door, and Mr. Miller's voice came through. "Gwendolyn? Is everything all right? Are you well?"

Relief washed over her as she came slowly back to the door and undid the two deadbolts there. She opened the door a bit and found Mr. Miller standing in the hallway. "I'm all right, Mr. Miller. Thank you for your help."

His brow was furrowed with concern. "I told him

that you have nothing to do with the business that Madeline is in and that you just clean laundry and can barely make rent. He seemed to believe me, but he wasn't happy about it."

"I'm sorry you had to get involved at all, Mr. Miller."

He shook his head and rubbed the back of his neck. "I don't know if you should be involved in this either. Madeline is doing work that's going to do nothing but bring her trouble, and it looks like some of that trouble is going to spill over your direction, too."

Frowning, Gwendolyn couldn't do more than just nod, as the lump formed in her throat again.

"Well, all right. I know it's not any of my business, but I kind of think of you like a daughter—since you're about my daughter's age. And I don't want anything bad to happen to a good Christian girl like you."

She swallowed hard and barely managed to whisper, "Thank you, Mr. Miller."

He nodded, waved, and disappeared back into his apartment across the hall. Gwendolyn's shoulders fell as she hooked her bible into the crook of her arm and set the deadbolts again on the door. Mr. Miller was right. Her feelings about not being able to stay here any longer were also right. But where would she go? What would she do?

Like the strength in her legs had completely run out, she collapsed into the kitchen chair and set her bible down on the newspaper sitting in front of her. Bowing her head, she closed her eyes and prayed, tears seeping from her eyes as she did so. Nothing in life was going the way that it was supposed to. Winter was coming, and things would only get worse. What was she supposed to do now? She beseeched God for a long while, until she smelled burning. Her soup was ruined. She got up after saying "Amen" and swiping the tears from her face. Honestly, she wasn't hungry anymore, anyway. Pulling the pan from the stove, she set it on a towel on the countertop to cool before she could throw out the contents and clean the pot.

Then with a sigh, she sat back down on the chair again, her elbow pushing aside the Bible from the newspaper. There her eyes were drawn to an advertisement looking for mail-order brides to travel out west where there was a shortage of women. The office in Denver was looking to match career women back east who were well-educated to match with educated men with strong prospects in the west.

Pulling her gaze away, she shook her head. No.

She could never become a mail-order bride. That wasn't something she should consider at all. Heading off on a train to go meet a stranger... no, not just meet him. Marry him. She shook her head again. That was just crazy.

But for some reason her gaze was drawn back to the advertisement again. God often asked those who loved Him to do crazy, unheard of things. Was this His will? Was she really going to go run off to Denver, Colorado? It was hundreds if not thousands of miles away from everything she knew.

What was it that she knew? What was so great about it? She lived in a hovel with a friend who had become a lady of the night, and was pressuring her to become one, too. And even if Gwendolyn continued to refuse, it seemed that Madeline's lifestyle was having repercussions for Gwendolyn, as well. She let out a breath and pushed a flyaway from her bun back behind her ear. Then she looked closer at the advertisement.

Something sparked in her heart and she knew that she was being called to answer the advertisement. She let out a deep breath. "Are you sure, Lord?"

Then she rubbed the goose flesh down on her arms when they rose up. What a stupid question to ask the God of the universe. As if He was ever unsure of anything. She couldn't help but huff a laugh at herself. Then she took the paper and tore off the advertisement. She stuffed it into the front cover of her bible and then stood, turned around, and began packing her carpet bag.

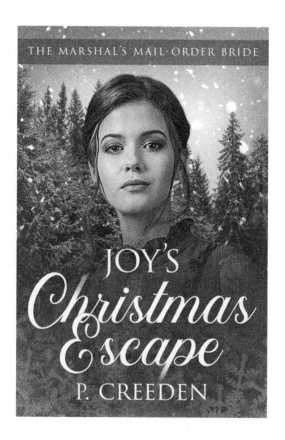

With danger and redemption swirling around them, can an unlikely Christmas miracle still be found in Virginia City?

Schoolteacher Joy Stewart has never been lucky. Her father died before she was born. Her mother left her in the care of her grandmother so that she could get remarried and move far away. So when her grandmother succumbs to illness, her debtors come to call. And one of them has his eyes set on Joy to be his bride as payment for his debt. That bad luck just seems to be compounding on Joy—what she needs is a Christmas Miracle, and her grandmother has put a plan in the works...

Marshal Jack Bolling has found himself in want of a nanny. With the death of his sister and her husband in a tragic accident, he has now come into possession of his twin niece and nephew of four years old. For over a month he's had no luck in locating an appropriate nanny for them—at least not on his salary and what a marshal can afford. But then his good friend, Pastor North has the idea that perhaps Jack should be looking for a wife instead? The thought of that sends chills down Jack's spine, but when he end's up putting the twins' lives in danger due to his job, he wonders what choice he has. But can he even dare to hope that he'd be lucky enough to find a wife so close to Christmastime?

Get your copy of Joy's Christmas Escape!

And check out the rest of the books in The Marshal's Mail-Order Bride series:

THE MARSHAL'S MAIL ORDER BRIDE ~ Eight brides each find themselves in a compromising situation – and the only way out is to escape west and become a mail-order bride. But will trouble follow them? Good thing they are heading into the arms of a law man. Each bride has a different, stand alone story ~ Read each one and don't miss out!

FIRST CHAPTER OF JOY'S CHRISTMAS ESCAPE

"What's that over there?" Sam the barber asked, pointing toward the east.

A storm had just passed over, and Marshal Jack Bolling had been looking west, toward the sunset where the sky was already brightening for the moments just before sunset. The slightest drizzle still hung in the air, dripping a drop or two now and then. But following Sam's question, he looked the direction the man pointed.

Against the still stormy sky, a dark column of smoke rose, darker than the clouds above it. He frowned. "Looks like a fire."

He picked up a jog and headed toward the livery, calling over his shoulder, "Get the men of town together. We may be needing a bucket brigade."

"You bet!" Sam yelled back.

Jack knew he could count on Sam to get most of the men in town on board to help. No one wanted a fire to spread. He couldn't pinpoint exactly where the fire was, but he imagined that it was a bit outside of Virginia City, possibly in one of the farm homes nearby. When he reached the livery, he hollered inside. "Clyde! Grab as many buckets as you can. There's a fire!"

Clyde came out of a horse's stall with a pitchfork, his eyes wide. "Which way?'

"East," Jack answered, as he stepped to the paddock just outside the livery and grabbed hold of his chestnut gelding, Red. Quickly, he swung a saddle on the horse's back and cinched the girth loosely. No matter what kind of hurry he was in, Jack had a promise to keep with Red. He'd never tighten the cinch too fast and would always give the gelding time to adjust before pulling the leather strap hard. He then reached over the horse's head and pulled the bridle up over his ears. Once it was buckled in place, Jack led Red forward a couple of steps before pulling the cinch strap tight. He tied it in its knot and then shoved a foot into the stirrup and swung into the saddle. Before he was all the way up, Red was already moving forward, seeming to sense the urgency in Jack's movements.

Once in the saddle, Jack reined the horse to the east. He didn't know how long Red had been sitting since he'd dropped him off at the livery a couple hours before the storm came. Early October storms still had remnants of the power of those in the late summer. Fall couldn't come soon enough. He was sick of the hail and lightning. He huffed. It might've been lightning that caused this fire. Even as he started letting his gelding jog in the direction of the smoke, he sent up a quick, silent prayer that no one would be hurt.

The cloud over the black column was already thick and wide and continuing to spread. It was worrisome to see the clouds like that. Likely it meant that the fire had been raging for at least a little while. But no one would have noticed because the storm had kept everyone inside. Jack himself had been in the barber shop getting a shave to pass the time while he waited out whatever the storm would bring.

There hadn't been a lot of rain in this one, but the hail had been about dime-sized and the thunder had rumbled for at least an hour. He thought back to the one big crack that had shaken the building about forty-five minutes ago and suddenly he wondered if this fire might have been the result of the lightning that had caused that peal. After a short bit, his horse picked up a lope. He rounded the bend and in the distance it was becoming easier to determine exactly where the fire might be coming from. And immediately his heart sank.

The lope became a gallop as he opened Red up and asked him to move faster. The smoke was coming from a location much too close to his old family home—his sister's house. Another prayer went up as he groaned. No. Please don't let her be hurt. Or the twins. The two cherub faces flashed before his mind as his stomach squeezed, and he felt a little nauseous.

Unfortunately, the closer he got to the fire, the more certain it seemed that it was coming from Penelope and her family's house. As he galloped closer, he found a small crowd of neighbors already trying to form a bucket brigade from the well to the house, but there were only a few of them. A measure of relief hit Jack when he saw his little niece and nephew standing together in their nightgowns with a young woman. They were safe. Thank the Lord.

He ran straight for them, pulling up his horse

when he was a few yards away and launching himself from the saddle. "Penelope!"

The young woman stood and turned about, and that's when he realized the young woman wasn't his sister, it was Grace Scott from across the street. He blinked, his pace faltering for a moment as he took in more of his surroundings. It was then he noticed two bodies that had been covered by blankets nearby. And the world tilted and spun as Grace started speaking to him, but for the ringing in his ears, he couldn't hear a word she said.

Dressed in black, Joy stood before a freshly dug grave, watching as the gravediggers began shoveling in the dirt that would bury her beloved grand-mother. How could it be so sunny out when the only family that Joy had in the world—the only person who'd ever loved her—was being buried? Geese flew overhead making such a racket in their migrations, that Joy's own sobs were drowned out. The late October breeze blew in the treetops, sending multi-colored leaves to swirl around her and the gravesite.

In the past, Joy had always loved the fall. It was a blessed respite from the hot summers in Memphis.

It was when school started for the children, and when Joy had the most hope for the coming school year. But that had been shadowed by the illness that plagued her grandmother over the last few months. Even though her grandmother had told her that everything was all right and that she should continue to go to the schoolhouse and work, Joy had known better. She regretted listening to her grandmother's pretense. Instead of starting the school year, she should have stayed at home and taken care of her grandmother. Maybe then, her grandmother wouldn't have died so soon. Maybe then, Joy would have been able to take care of her and spend more time with her at least. But she knew that she couldn't have given up the income from teaching at the school. Modest though it was, it helped pay for the medicine to keep her grandmother from the pains she had.

"Miss Stewart," a deep, gruff voice said from behind her.

Swiping at the tears on her cheeks, she turned around, preparing to give a false smile to whoever might be waiting to give her their condolences. But instead, she found a man who was standing much closer to her than she'd expected, a taller, larger man than she'd ever seen before, and she had to tilt her neck back just to meet gazes with him. She furrowed her brow in confusion. "Um... yes. I'm Miss Stewart."

He nodded, taking hold of her elbow. "I knew as much. Come with me, please."

Immediately he started guiding her away from the gravesite. Although the man had said please, it felt like a platitude. There was no denying the brute. When she grew slow to follow, his grip on her elbow tightened, causing her chest to tighten in fear as well. "Where are you taking me?"

"Just come along."

She swallowed hard, her feet catching her as she almost stumbled. Still, she followed knowing she didn't have much choice but to do as he said. If she tried to stop, the reprobate would likely drag her. They continued to make their way down the hill toward the gravel road that lead out of the yard when a black stagecoach pulled by two dark horses came into view. For some reason, the sight of it caused the hairs on the back of Joy's neck to stand on end. It was as if the grim reaper himself might be hiding behind the dark curtain in the window. Her heart raced in her chest as she was pulled out a halt just outside the door of the carriage.

The brute who had been manhandling her kept a hand on her elbow but stepped forward and knocked on the side of the carriage. "Mr. Pomeroy, this here is Miss Joy Stewart."

Her stomach began to quiver and even though there was a slight chill in the breeze, she'd begun to perspire. What did these people want with her?

With a quick swish, the curtain on the carriage opened, revealing a balding, spectacled man with beady, black eyes. He looked her up and down and quirked an eyebrow. Then he smiled, showing pronounced bucked teeth that reminded her of a rat or beaver. "So you're the lone heir to Madam Henrietta Stewart?"

Frowning, but feeling only slightly less afraid, Joy refused to answer. What did this man want with her, and how would he know anything about her or her grandmother?

Then the brute at her elbow shook her. "Answer Mr. Pomeroy, woman."

"Now, now, Big Donald. Don't be too rough with the lady, and show her the respect enough to call her miss. After all, she is a schoolteacher, not a saloon girl."

"Yes, sir." The scoundrel lightened his grip on her arm, but only slightly. "Excuse me, Miss, but please answer Mr. Pomeroy."

Joy swallowed hard, unsure of what was going

on. How did this man even know her name, much less her occupation? Why did it seem that this man knew so much about her, but she'd never heard of him or seen him before in her life? What was going on? Her vision crowded with black dots, and she feared she might faint. But she bit the inside of her cheek in desperation to get a hold of herself. The last thing she wanted to do was faint in front of these villains. The pain in her cheek was sharp but bearable, and it helped to scatter the dots that had threatened to take hold of her. Coppery blood trickled upon her tongue, and she managed to regain her composure. Her hands fisted at her sides, and she yanked her elbow from the brute's grip. Anger overwhelmed the fear she'd felt moments before. "What is this all about, sir? Why would this... this ruffian drag me all the way down here to meet with someone I do not know?"

The smile upon the man's lips didn't change, but his eyes flashed a bit with something like amusement. "Are you angry now, Miss Stewart? I apologize for my man's mishandling of you. It was disrespectful. I'll ask that he not lay a hand upon you again, if that will make you happy."

His sudden sweetness was more unnerving than his appearance. She rubbed at her elbow and didn't say anything again. She wasn't certain just how to respond to this man. But his speech did deflate the anger she'd been building.

The stranger shrugged and pushed open the carriage door. Joy had to step backwards to keep the man from invading her space. He placed a bowler upon his head; the felt hat was only a few shades darker than the brown suit that he wore. He stood at eye-level with her, a small, mousy man who seemed to be the opposite of the heathen who'd grabbed her by the elbow before, but somehow more dangerous. Her hair stood on end again while he looked her up and down again, taking measure of her.

Her voice shook as she asked, "Mr. Pomeroy, was it? Could I ask what business you have with me?"

His brow lifted again. "You are a pretty one, aren't you. It shouldn't be surprising. Even as an old crone, you could tell that Ms. Henrietta Stewart was quite the looker back in her day. My father had said as such. It was one of the reasons that he was so quick to give her the loans that she asked for."

Joy frowned. "What loans?"

"What loans?" The man chuckled and shook his head. Then he began pacing around her in a circle. "Surely you're not going to play ignorant with me, are you? I already know that you're not stupid. After all, you are a schoolteacher."

"How... how do you know I'm a schoolteacher," she asked, feeling a bit breathless.

"I make it my business to know as much as I can about those who owe me debts. And since Ms. Henrietta Stewart is now no longer able to pay her debts, the burden, unfortunately is passed on to you, Miss Joy Stewart, as the former's only living heir."

The shiver that had started in Joy's stomach began to quake in earnest. "What... what do you mean? I have no earthly idea what you are talking about." She hated that she couldn't stop the shaking or remove the slight whine out of her voice.

The man stopped directly in front of her, narrowing his beady black eyes and taking her chin in his hand. "Whether you want to play dumb or actually are dumb enough to think that your grandmother could live at the house where you have made your home the last fifteen years without employment or indebtedness, it doesn't matter. The truth of the matter is that your grandmother owes my family two thousand four hundred dollars, and I've come to collect."

A JOURNEY FOR LILY

When Lily Browne's father loses his job at the bank, he decides to make the journey out west, to claim land for cheap in Oregon. And when Lily hears of the need for school teachers out there, she decides that she must go too. There's only one problem. Even though Lily is barely nineteen, the wagon master demands that she cannot accompany the train without being wed. But she can't be a school teacher if she's married...

Wayne Cody became a felon by accident when he was fifteen. After serving his time, he was released to find out that he has no family, and no more than five dollars to his name. He doesn't know much about anything other than guns, horses, and cattle, so he attempts to get hired by a wagon train to help several families make it to Oregon to claim land. If he can somehow earn enough money, he can claim land for himself, too. Then, Mr. Browne makes him an offer he can't refuse.

Get your copy of A Journey for Lily!

And check out the rest of the books in The Reluctant Wagon Train Bride Series:

"The west is too wild for an unwed woman. If you want to ride on my wagon train and make it to Oregon, you'll need to find yourself a husband."

THE RELUCTANT WAGON TRAIN BRIDE ~ Twenty brides find themselves in a compromising situation. They have to get married in order to travel to Oregon on their wagon train. Each story in the series is a clean, standalone romance. Will the bride end up falling in love with her reluctant husband? Or will she get an annulment when they reach Oregon? Each bride has a different story ~ Read each one and don't miss out!

FIRST CHAPTER OF A JOURNEY FOR LILY

April 1854

JEFFERSON CITY MISSOURI

Wayne Cody blew out a long breath and pressed the barrel of his revolver under his chin. The late April sun beat down on him from overhead and the rock he sat upon was almost too hot to bear through his dungarees. Sweat beaded on his forehead and made a trail down the side of his face before dripping off his jaw. "Oh, God," he groaned, but was unsure what else to say.

He closed his eyes, his finger moving from the guard to the trigger and then he caught himself holding his breath again. A fly buzzed around his head, and he had the fleeting thought that the fly was likely to eat well soon. That brought other morbid thoughts to mind about maggots and other creatures that might find his body once he pulled the trigger. But when would a human find him?

He sat outside the limits of the town of Jefferson City, not too far off the main roadway, but other than the road, there wasn't much more than stretches of barren wilderness in all directions. It might be a few days before someone would wander off the trail far enough to find him. Would the livery keeper look for him when the horse Wayne had bought for three dollars showed back up at the livery? He doubted it.

Another breath expelled from his lungs; another droplet of sweat made a trail down the side of his face. A horse whinnied in the distance, causing the one whose reins he held to wicker softly in return. Would the person see his horse? Perhaps if Wayne waited just a bit longer, his gunshot would catch the attention of the traveler heading his direction. Then maybe he'd save himself from being eaten by whatever creature took a fancy to his carcass.

That made him huff a small laugh even though it wasn't funny. His heart rate had slowed. How long was he going to sit there before pulling the trigger? The steel in his palm was heating up from the sun blazing upon the rest of the gun. Maybe he should just pull the thing away, at least until the rider came closer. Somehow the thought of doing that made him feel weaker, more cowardly.

Or was he taking the coward's way out already?

Maybe. But would it really be brave at all to keep on living in a world where he had no one—not one family member to speak of? Not one friend. No job prospects, as a felon. And hardly more than a dollar to his name now that he'd spent three on a horse?

If only.

If only he hadn't drunk that whiskey on that day when he was fifteen. If only he hadn't gone along with it when Joe and Bill had decided to go turkey shooting after they'd been drinking. If only Bill hadn't let off a shot too close to the Reed's home. If only that bullet hadn't hit Mrs. Reed and injured her gravely. If only Mrs. Reed hadn't died before the trial started. If only those two brothers hadn't pointed the finger at him.

Then, maybe he would have been at home helping his mother around the farm so that she hadn't died two years before the end of his ten-year sentence. And prison had been hard on him. There were people who called the Missouri Penitentiary the bloodiest acres in the state. And they wouldn't be wrong. Only the strongest men survived. The weaker men ended up dead or enslaved in manners unbefitting to mention. Wayne had had to fight so that he wouldn't end up in one of those two conditions. Back then he'd fought for his life, but he'd paid for it in other ways. He'd lost a molar on the left side in one fight, ended up with a scar across his right cheek that had healed a bright shade of pink and caused that part of his face to sink in a little bit. And his now crooked nose had been broken three times. Getting employment had become impossible for him. With just a look at him, he was turned away before he could get one word out of his mouth.

"Oh, Lord, I'm sorry..." he groaned again.

The world would be better off without him. Living in the prison had been hell enough, surely the hell that was saved for people like him who took their own lives couldn't be any worse. A tear welled in his eye and slipped out from under his lid, joining the sweat trails to his chin. Or maybe God would have mercy on him since he'd only been in that situation because of an accident and an accusation, even though he'd been innocent the whole time.

Not that anyone believed him.

His shoulders slumped. And he could just about hear the hoof beats behind him. Time was up. He needed to go ahead and get this over with before he lost his resolve. Sitting up straighter, he took a deep breath and held it for half a moment, preparing to pull the trigger on his exhale.

"Cody? Is that you?" a familiar voice called out from behind him.

Confusion and embarrassment both struck Wayne in equal measures as his eyes snapped open. He yanked the revolver from his chin and stood quickly, wiping his face on his sleeve before spinning on his heel. He swiped at his face once more hoping there'd be no trace of his tears.

Sitting upon a chestnut mare, Mason Bradley offered a gap-toothed grin and pushed his straw hat up a little off his forehead. "I thought that was you. Didn't you leave the pen three days ago? I thought you'd be long gone by now."

Clearing his dry throat, Wayne looked down, dusting off his dungarees in a moment to gain composure. Then he shook his head. "Got no where to go."

Bradley's brow lifted. "Really? No where?"

A lump formed in Wayne's throat, and he shook his head.

"Why don't you come with me then? I'm heading up to Independence. My uncle there is a supplier of cattle and oxen for fools trying to make it on the trail to Oregon. It's easy money and he's always hiring a cowboy or two. I'll put in a good word for you."

Wayne blinked at the man and swallowed hard. "Why would you do that?"

Bradley shrugged. "I just thought with a mug like yours, even the railroad wouldn't hire you. Call it pity if you want." He sat up straighter in the saddle and reined his horse back to the road. "If you don't want to come, then don't come," he called out from behind him as he started trotting away.

His heart suddenly racing, Wayne pulled the bay gelding he'd bought by the rein to draw him closer and then shoved his foot into the stirrup and mounted while the horse had already started away at a trot after his buddy from the livery. Wayne barely managed to right himself in the saddle and shove his felt hat upon his head before catching up to Bradley.

Bradley eyed him with a half-cocked grin and nodded. "Ain't you glad that you helped me out that one time in the yard?"

Even though he nodded, Wayne's brows scrunched as he tried to remember. He and Bradley had always been on friendly terms with each other, but never quite friends. And Wayne didn't remember helping the man out, but it didn't mean that he hadn't in some manner. Fights were frequent in the yard, and sometimes he'd just find himself involved.

Regardless, as they rode their horses toward the northwest, Wayne sent up a small silent prayer. It wasn't much more than just a thanks. But he hoped that God, at least, knew what he meant.

LILY BROWNE SQUINTED OVER HER SPECTACLES OUT the window of the Independence hotel, trying to make out the shapes of the men on the street. Her father had worn his smart, gray suit and she had hoped to make him out by the color. Her spectacles helped her to read and to make out faces when they were close, but even her vision farther away seemed to be getting worse. She didn't want to bother her father with that small thing now, so she decided to live with it until they made their way out to the west.

A small cough came from the bed next to the

window, and Lily turned toward the sound. Her nine-year-old brother, Thomas, sat up from the bed slowly, his pallor making his eyes seem an impossible shade of blue. She scrunched her brows as she stood, setting her book and spectacles on the table before she came over, resting a hand upon his forehead to see if he was feverish.

"Do you think I could go outside today?" His eyes met hers, and his voice sounded a bit dry.

She reached for the pitcher by the table and poured him a glass of water. "If you're feeling strong, we could go down to the dining room and get you a bite of something to eat. And if you're still up for it, we can take a short walk along the street."

A broad smile spread across his lips as he threw aside his covers and took the glass from her. He took a quick sip and tried to return it to her hands.

She shook her head and pushed the glass back toward him. "Drink it all, please. It will make your throat feel better."

He huffed, but did as he was asked and downed the whole glass. This time, though instead of handing it back to her, he set it down on the table with a clink. "There. Now can I go get ready?"

"Of course," she said with a smile and stepped back toward the window to give her brother some privacy while he changed behind the screen. Again, she picked up the spectacles and looked through and over them a few more times, trying to determine which method to use when trying to see farther away. Finally, she decided that she could see better without the spectacles when trying to see as far as the street. Her brother shuffled behind her. He'd lost so much weight, his clothes were at least a size or two too big now. The sickness had taken away his appetite and how could her brother heal if he didn't eat well? Even though her father talked almost constantly about the adventures they'd be having in this trip across the Wild West, she knew their reason for going was two-fold. So that her father could gain land and employment, and so that her brother could get the air that he needed to get better.

"I'm ready," Thomas finally called out with a voice that was more chipper than she'd heard in the last few days.

"Okay," Lily said as she turned around, "but I want to see you eat at least half your eggs before I even think about letting you go for that walk. And a few bites of toast and oatmeal too."

Her brother groaned but nodded his head. "As long as I can go for a walk outside, I'll eat twice that much."

A smile pulled on Lilly's lip. She'd love to see him eat as much as he said. Together the two of them started out the door of their room and down the hallway to the stairs. If her brother could make it down the flight of stairs to the dining room without having to catch his breath, Lily would count that as a blessing all in itself.

LOVE WESTERN ROMANCE?

Join the Historical Western Romance Readers on Facebook to hear about more great books, play fun games, and often win prizes!

Printed in Great Britain
by Amazon